OLD VIC PREFACES

'If I profane with my unworthiest hand . . .'

JULIET: Claire Bloom   ROMEO: Alan Badel

HUGH HUNT

OLD VIC

PREFACES

Shakespeare and the Producer

GREENWOOD PRESS, PUBLISHERS
WESTPORT, CONNECTICUT

Library of Congress Cataloging in Publication Data

Hunt, Hugh, 1911-
  Old Vic prefaces.

  Reprint of the 1954 ed.
  1. Shakespeare, William, 1564-1616--Stage history--
1800-   2. Shakespeare, William, 1564-1616--Criticism
and interpretation. 3. London. Old Vic Theatre.
I. Title.
PR3106.H8 1973   822.3'3   72-6197
ISBN 0-8371-6460-5

First published in 1954 by Routledge & Kegan Paul, London

Reprinted with the permission of Routledge & Kegan Paul Ltd.

Reprinted by Greenwood Press,
a division of Williamhouse-Regency Inc.

First Greenwood Reprinting 1973
Second Greenwood Reprinting 1974

Library of Congress Catalog Card Number 72-6197

ISBN 0-8371-6460-5

Printed in the United States of America

CONTENTS

ILLUSTRATIONS

PREFACE

THESE prefaces were intended as introductions to the Shakespeare productions for which I was responsible at the Old Vic between the years 1949 and 1953. As such they were read to the casts which were to perform the plays, and were not intended to be analysed in the study. But for the purposes of this volume I have not thought fit to alter their style, believing their interest to lie more in their original intention as production blueprints than as dramatic essays.

They do not aspire to the dignity of literary criticism, nor is it their function to uncover new facts about the plays they treat. They represent the personal approach of a producer to his work. Often they omit the most striking points of characterization and of scholastic discovery, not with the intention of discarding such points, but because they are either obvious or have been sufficiently stressed. If these prefaces have any interest to others, it is an example of a producer's approach to an acted play, as distinct from a scholar's approach to a printed play.

The approach of a producer to a play—providing such approach is interpretative and not imitative—is ephemeral. It is based on the impression the play makes on him at a specific moment. Such an impression is more emotional than logical, though reason must not be supposed to be absent. For, though the approach may be said to be personal to the producer, the final production must take into account not only the views of author, players and designer, but such necessary and mundane matters as how much money is available, how much time can be given to rehearsals, what size is the stage and what equipment it possesses. These and other circumstances make the theatre an ephemeral art; to attempt to revive a production is nearly always disappointing. However carefully we may preserve our prompt-books, lighting plots, designs and models, a production like a painting can be copied, but not relived.

These prefaces, then, do not set out to standardize the approach to Shakespeare's plays, nor even to suggest what the approach should be. I have sometimes been asked to lend a prompt-book to a group of amateurs who wished to produce a play in the same way. I have always refused such requests; not out of desire to preserve proprietary rights, but because imitation destroys the individuality of approach which is the life of the theatre. These prefaces do not even represent my fixed views on the approach to the plays; I have produced *King Lear* three times at wide intervals and each time I have adopted a different approach—the one that seemed to be right at the time. It is a measure of a playwright's genius, as it is of a painter, a sculptor, or a musician, that not only do his works inspire each one of us differently, but some new feature, angle or perspective, some different colour or atmosphere will be made clear to us each time we contemplate them afresh. Lesser men allow but one interpretation of their work.

This variety of interpretation, which results from a work of art, can also be its misfortune, and monstrous abortions of misplaced imagination have been, and will be, perpetrated on the stage in the name of creative interpretation. It is the task of the producer to keep his imagination within bounds and to do so he must have a full measure of understanding, knowledge and love of his text. Nor must this sympathetic approach be confined only to the text of the play, it must extend to the very existence, creed and personality of the author himself, in so far as these can be known and felt by him.

The approach of a producer to the text of a Shakespeare play differs from that of a scholar. Literary criticism is abstract and largely impersonal, for the scholar must base his assertions on fact and his conjectures must be hedged with authority. The producer, however, has not the benefit of footnotes;

he can give neither authority for, nor explanation of, his assertions. His approach is an imaginative approach, his interpretation is hedged by circumstances. However much he may and should use the scholarship of the literary critic to provide him with background and knowledge, it is his imagination and his judgement that will finally affect his interpretation. For the producer has to take into account a primary factor of the stage which is unnecessary and unbecoming to the scholar —the live performance of the play to a contemporary audience.

Imagination and creation are necessary to production, but they must be bounded by good taste and understanding of the author's intention. These qualities of imagination and creation separate the producer from the scholar and often earn him the strictures of the critic. It is of interest to the scholar to know that the character of Moth in *Love's Labour's Lost* is intended as a satirical sketch of the poet Nashe, but what is the producer to do with this character if the eccentricities of the original are unknown to the audience? The joke is as dead as would be Hermione Gingold's sketch of a disgruntled Girl-Guide at the court of Elizabeth I. The principles of Shakespearian production must be to balance literary appreciation with entertainment, for Shakespeare wrote his plays for an audience, not for the erudite satisfaction of the reader, the scholar and the critic.

Now the taste of an audience is a changeable affair and, like the successful couturier, the producer of Shakespeare must lead and satisfy public taste. The only way to succeed is to rely on his own instincts, rather than copy the work of others. In doing so he must expect to meet with many failures, for the elements he has to balance are both various and delicate. He is not dealing with paint and canvas, nor with chisel and stone, but with human beings.

Though much has been written about the art of the actor, little is known about the craft of the producer. How does the producer learn this craft? There is no school for the producer, no accepted maxims to guide him, no acknowledged ladder of promotion. To each preface I have added a postscript with the intention of bringing out some point that arose either in rehearsal or performance, and which illustrates the type of problems that confront a producer and the sort of mistakes he can make. It is my hope that these simple hints may be of some assistance to those who aspire to undertake this difficult task.

The style of production will alter from producer to producer and from year to year, and nothing seems more out of date than accounts of past productions or the photographs which embellish the autobiographies of our actors and actresses. But since the stage is an ephemeral art, it is good that we still have these records; from them as well as from intelligent criticism we can glean something of the intention and atmosphere of past interpretations. For those of you who did not see the productions for which these prefaces were written, there may be such a gleaning; for those who did, there may be a reliving of an experience.

The interpretation of a play is by no means the sole conception of a producer. It would, however, be fair to say that the combined operation of a play's production originates from his blueprint. These blueprints, then, are dedicated to the players, designers, musicians, stage-managers, costumiers, scenic painters, makers of scenery and properties, masters of fencing and arrangers of dancing through whose co-operation and loyalty the plays were performed.

1953

LOVE'S LABOUR'S LOST

LOVE'S LABOUR'S LOST
Old Vic Theatre Company
New Theatre. 11th October 1949

FERDINAND, *King of Navarre*	MICHAEL ALDRIDGE
LONGAVILL	GORDON WHITING
DUMAIN	NIGEL STOCK
BEROWNE	MICHAEL REDGRAVE
DULL, *A Constable*	PAUL ROGERS
COSTARD, *A Clown*	GEORGE BENSON
DON ARDIANO DE ARMADO	BALIOL HOLLOWAY
MOTH, *Page to Armado*	BRIAN SMITH
JAQUENETTA	ROSALIND BOXALL
BOYET	WALTER HUDD
THE PRINCESS OF FRANCE	ANGELA BADDELEY
MARIA	JANE WENHAM
KATHERINE	YVONNE MITCHELL
ROSALINE	DIANA CHURCHILL
A FORESTER	LEO MCKERN
HOLOFERNES	MARK DIGNAM
SIR NATHANIEL	MILES MALLESON
MERCADE, *A Messenger*	RICHARD WALTER

ATTENDANTS, PEDANTS AND HUNTSMEN:
DELIA WILLIAMS, COLIN CAMPBELL, RODNEY DIAK, WILLIAM EEDLE, LESLIE GLAZER, NORMAN WELSH, RICHARD WALTER.

Scenery and costumes designed by Berkeley Sutcliffe. Music composed and arranged by Herbert Menges.

2

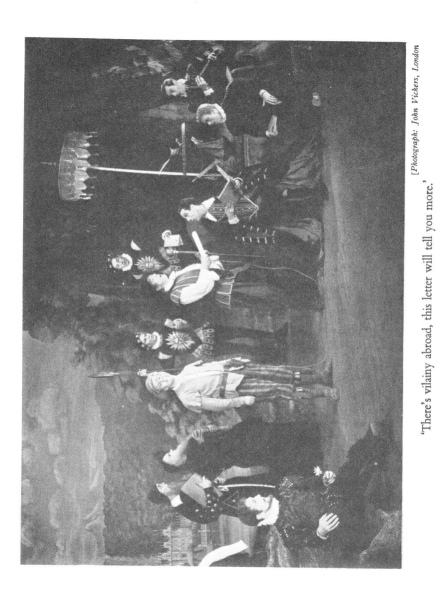

'There's villainy abroad, this letter will tell you more.'

BEROWNE: Michael Redgrave   COSTARD: George Benson

DULL: Paul Rogers   THE KING: Michael Aldridge

[*Photograph: John Vickers, London*]

HOLOFERNES: Mark Dignam

SIR NATHANIEL: Miles Malleson

BEROWNE: Michael Redgrave

ROSALINE: Diana Churchill

LOVE'S LABOUR'S LOST

Love's Labour's Lost is an early play written somewhere between *The Comedy of Errors* and *Romeo and Juliet*. It has been suggested it was written for a private performance in 1593, when an outbreak of plague caused the closure of the London theatres. At all events, the style of the play would be more likely to appeal to a sophisticated than to a popular audience. Errors and duplications in the text may be due to later revisions prior to the first public performance in London which must have taken place before 1598 when the text was printed.

From our point of view such historical questions are immaterial, except in so far as they affect the play's style, and the significance of the satire contained in it. I propose to deal with these aspects of *Love's Labour* before proceeding to an analysis of the characters; they may help you to harmonize your individual characterizations with the atmosphere and intention of the production.

Let me state at the outset that this production sets out to be neither archaic nor experimental, in the belief that the play itself with the sweetness of its verbal music, its rich costume and youthful outlook makes, despite obvious weaknesses, a special appeal to the romantic in us all.

The date of this play relates it directly to Shakespeare's early sonnet period, to the period of *Venus and Adonis* and to 'Sweet Mr. Shakespeare'. The author is fascinated by the richness of his native tongue, by the conceits of court language, by the lively interplay of wit and by the wealth of Renaissance imagery. The young Shakespeare, fresh from the sober life of provincial Stratford, is here seen embarking on his career as a playwright, as yet ignorant of the darker dreams to come. But if there are no dark dreams in *Love's Labour*, there is, as in all his comedies, a gentle melancholy at the inevitable passing of youth, which is a distinctive feature of its atmosphere. Our young author was revelling in his newly found freedom in London, in the 'taffeta phrases' and 'three-piled hyperboles' of his fellow poets, in his personal success not only with his fellow-players, but with 'certain persons of note'—the most eminent and cultured noblemen in the land. For him the door to fame and favour had sprung open and we cannot wonder if the product of a provincial grammar school, the son of a middle-class shop-keeper, was intoxicated as he basked in the sunshine of the darlings of Elizabeth's court—the handsome Earl of South-ampton and the brilliant Earl of Essex. What glory lay ahead of him with such patrons! With his newly proven ability he could show himself worthy of his mother's noble family, retrieve his father's fallen fortunes, lay claim to a gentleman's coat of arms and, if fortune favoured him at the box office, purchase some day a fine house in Stratford to which he might return as an envied and respected citizen. This young ambitious Shakespeare had not reached the mature humanity of *Twelfth Night*, nor been troubled by the dark imagery of *Macbeth*. He had not been scared by the tearing passions and bitterness of *Othello, Lear* and *Timon*, nor had he found the final serenity of *The Tempest*. The author of *Love's Labour* was a young man and therein lies the play's charm. It is a young man's poem written in the early summer of manhood, when the only cloud on the horizon was the gentle sadness of passing youth; the recurrent theme that 'Summer's lease hath all too short a date'. It is a poem written to please the cultured young bloods of Elizabeth's court—the highly-educated, imaginative, ambi-tious, fascinating swordsmen, scholars, poets and soldiers who surrounded the person of the Faery Queen. But despite its jewelled jests, its play of wit against wit, its rich imagery and its intricate word-play, *Love's Labour's Lost* remains the work of a country lad who had not forgotten the fields of Warwickshire, nor the small town life and gossip of Stratford-on-Avon. The language is shot through with the imagery of—

> 'Daisies pied, and violets blue,
> And lady-smocks all silver white'

of 'blossoms floating on the wanton air'. Through this Warwickshire Arcadia walk the village schoolmaster with his horn-book, the curate with his nasal intonations, the yokel with his earthy jests. Through these groves sound the music-clamour of hound and horn; whilst overhead it is not the olive trees of Navarre that shelter us from the sun, but the leafy shade of our English oaks. It is a poem and must be spoken as such. It is verbal music, the music of rhyme and tripping blank verse, and from this cornucopia of singing words are drawn the threads from which the tapestry of the play is woven. Movement, gesture, music, scenery and costume must serve the poetry of the play; and our voices, which are the agents of poetry, must be our principal concern. In this play sound is often more important than sense. Meanings are sometimes obscure; we can frequently only understand and illustrate them by the style of our speech and our movements. Many of the local and contemporary witticisms have been lost, some so far that we have no recourse but to cut them as best we can. The important thing is that our approach to the text should be a stylish approach, rather than a psychological or naturalistic approach. We must treat the play as music. We must find its 'allegros', its 'andantes' and its 'scherzos'. That does not mean that characterization is unimportant, but it does mean that the speaking of the poetry, the playing of the music, the gracefulness of the movement, and the wearing of costume are all important; upon our success in mastering these will depend much of the success of the production.

The story of this play is simple enough. The young bloods of Navarre, headed by the King, take an oath of celibacy, they will wed themselves to learning, eschewing lovemaking, good eating, and the ordinary appetites of life for a period of three years. Their scheme is rudely interrupted by an embassy from the King of France, composed of the Princess and her ladies-in-waiting. The young gentlemen fall easy victims to the charms of their visitors and are, of course, embarrassed by the discovery of their mutual perfidy. Their wooing is, however, ended by the news of the death of the King of France. The Princess and her ladies, thereupon, ask their lovers to wait twelve months before renewing their suits. This is clearly a naïve plot; a more mature Shakespeare might have deepened it with a sub-plot, with psychological implications, with passion and universal significance, but our author had not yet learnt to give depth and inner meaning to his story, to make action depend on character and not character on action. Only to a very limited extent can we claim that the outcome of the story is the result of human virtues or frailties. We might say that the King of Navarre and his companions could have won their mistresses' favour more speedily, if they had been more sincere in their words, if they had not embarked on their foolish oath to eschew love-making. We might advance the theory that Don Armado's high-blown phrases land him into wedlock with the low-born wench Jaquenetta, but we would do better to recognize that character and plot have little to do with each other, and that *Love's Labour* has more the quality of a masque than of a play. This dramatic weakness must be turned by us into a virtue, and it can be so turned if we boldly emphasize the style, the youth and the atmosphere; if we speak it beautifully and treat it elegantly; if we acknowledge its lightness and emphasize its strength; and its strength is its lyrical quality, towards which all our efforts must be dedicated.

There is, however, one supreme moment in this story which must have considerable theatrical effect. This is the last scene, when the drama suddenly springs into life from the moment that Mercade brings his ill news which ends this summer flirtation. This scene contains the whole theme if we can use so strong a word in connexion with so slight an event. *Love's Labour's Lost*—the title itself indicates our theme. Shakespeare was obsessed during his early period with the brevity of youth and the hateful march of time—

> 'Time doth transfix the flourish set on youth
> And delves deep parallels in beauty's brow,
> Feeds on the rarities of nature's truth,
> And nothing stands but for his scythe to mow.'

The understanding of this motif is the key to our approach to the play. The short, gay period of courtship and raillery, of dance and song, of conceits of speech and pretences to learning is for him essential youth—the wonder of newly-won manhood, the little summer that is granted to each one of us before we are forced to face the responsibilities of living. Mercade comes like Time himself to turn the hour glass over. The King of France is dead, the laughter is over, the play acting finished, the courtship at an end. Suddenly the scene begins to cloud and we see that this light, seemingly pointless but endlessly charming, age of make-believe has now to face reality. It is through this approach—the gaiety and the sadness of youth—that we shall find compensation for the apparent naïveté of the story.

The Satire

In *Love's Labour* Shakespeare is poking gentle fun at the behaviour and language of a certain sect of his contemporaries —at the fashionable cult of Renaissance learning. This satire was, no doubt, primarily intended for the entertainment of the more cultured members of the audience, who would not only enjoy seeing 'the very age and body of the time' shown 'his form and pressure', but would revel in the thinly disguised allusions to the eccentricities of well-known personalities.

The main target of this satire is the affectation of language as exemplified in the 'taffeta phrases' of Armado, Berowne, Ferdinand, Dumain and Longavill and the elaborate love-making which is ridiculed by the Princess and her companions. But there are other affectations too—the Elizabethan habit of writing flowery letters and reports which is satirized in Don Armado's epistles, and the affectation of learning as practised by Holofernes, who can scarcely put two words of his native

7

language together without the benefit of a Latin quotation. The main affectations—those of language and love-making—are duly discredited by the events, and we are to suppose that the sufferers are cured by a twelve months' penance. It is evident, too, that Shakespeare had certain living models for his satire: the 'little academe' of Navarre may have been Walter Raleigh's 'School of Atheism', Don Armado may have been modelled on some Spanish visitor, Holofernes on some classical pedant, Moth on the poet, Tom Nashe. These satirical portraits can no longer affect us, indeed they make our task harder, for the flavour of satire is lost if we can no longer recognize the prototypes, or if the idiosyncrasies of behaviour are no longer practised amongst us. We must recognize that the topical flavour of this play has long since been buried by the dust of time. This is a serious problem from the point of view of a modern audience. It will be our task to try to overcome it by making the excesses of behaviour sufficiently amusing without having recourse to caricature or burlesque.

There is another slight complication in the satire of this play: Shakespeare himself was affected by the very affectation of language that he is so intent upon satirizing. Though he may use Berowne as his mouthpiece for denouncing the 'taffeta phrases', he is himself Berowne. His early sonnets as well as his early plays are bristling with 'taffeta phrases'. At this period of his life Shakespeare was in love with words, and in this play he is laughing at this same passion in others, much as Molière in *Le Misanthrope* is laughing at his own jealousy of his wife. To attempt to burlesque the jewelled conceits of the author's language would be to destroy the very threads from which the magic of his tapestry is woven.

The course that we must steer in following the satirical vein is to satirize insincerity—the insincerity of affected love-making, the insincerity of pretences to learning, the insincerity of oaths to eschew the normal, healthy life which Berowne-Shakespeare so heartily condemns. It was precisely this insincerity in love-making, this light way of treating the pains of love-sickness, which provoked the poem written in 1598 by Tofte after visiting a performance of *Love's Labour:*

Love's Labour Lost, I once did see a play
Ycleped so, so called to my pain.
Which I to hear to my small joy did stay,
Giving attendance on my froward dame:
   My misgiving mind presaging to me ill,
   Yet was I drawn to see it 'gainst my will.

This play, no play but plague was unto me,
For there I lost the Love I liked most;
And what to others seemed a jest to be,
I, that, in earnest, found unto my cost:
   To every one save me 'twas comical,
   Whilst tragic-like to me it did befall.

Each actor played in cunning-wise his part,
But chiefly those entrapped in Cupid's snare:
Yet all was feigned, 'twas not from the heart,
They seemed to grieve, but yet they felt no care:
   'Twas I that grief indeed did bear in breast,
   The others did but make a show in jest.

Yet neither feigning theirs, nor my mere truth,
Could make her once so much as for to smile:
Whilst she, despite of pity mild and ruth,
Did sit as scorning of my woes the while:
   Thus did she sit to see Love lose his Love,
   Like hardened rock that force nor power can move.

Thus we find an Elizabethan gentleman taking his girl friend to the theatre for much the same reasons as his descendant to-day will seek out the dark recesses of the cinema. What a mortification it must have been in this particular instance to find that an entertainment with such a suggestive title made fun of love itself.

We have suggested that *Love's Labour* with its stylistic language, its use of dance and music and its lack of depth of character is more akin to a masque than to a play, but what distinguishes it and compensates for any weakness it may contain is the atmosphere which Shakespeare, the lover of the English countryside, has woven around it. The key to this atmosphere is to be found in the rich summer feeling of the play to which the pastoral setting, the shade of the trees, the gradual fall of evening and the melancholy song of the owl contribute. We have already spoken of the play's theme—the passing of the springtime of youth—it is towards this ephemeral moment of man's life, which had so great an attraction for Shakespeare, that we must direct our attention when creating the mood in which to play it. I will, therefore, pass to the question of act division and location, through which the expression of this atmosphere will be aided.

The Division of the Play

The production will be divided into three parts each consisting of a single scene, so that the flow of the play will not be interrupted by frequent scene changes. There will, however, be two intervals.

Part I (Act I, Sc. 1: Act I, Sc. 2: Act II, Sc. 1)

This covers the initial phase of the play, introduces the background and the principal characters, except Holofernes and Sir Nathaniel, and leaves us with an interest in the development of the story and in the lively expectation of comedy. It is also a good break in the play's time sequence, for the incidents of Part I from the signing of the edict to the arrival of the embassy all take place on the same day.

Part II (Act III, Sc. 1: Act IV, Sc. 1: Act IV, Sc. 2: Act IV, Sc. 3: Act V, Sc. 1)

This is the hunting sequence, starting with the liberation of Costard and continuing up to, and including, the preparations for the Masque—a fitting climax to the day's sport. Again we are left with the expectation of comedy. We wait with interest the outcome of the joint courtship which the young bloods of Navarre plan after the uncomfortable discovery of their mutual perfidy. Part II takes place either on the day after Part I, or a few days later. The legal quibbles over the King of France's claim upon Navarre have been resolved, and the proceedings are to be wound up with festivity. All the events of this part take place within the space of six hours—namely midday to early evening.

Part III (Act V, Sc. 2)

This is the dénouement—an unexpected one—for the brittle comedy of love and make-belief is clouded over and the play ends in the mood of gentle melancholy about which we have spoken. Part III takes place on the same evening as the hunt, and when the curtain falls night has come.

Location of the Scenes

The whole play takes place in the park of Navarre. Let us imagine this castle of Navarre to be a little palace, built perhaps as a hunting lodge or summer residence, where the King can retire from the formalities of court life. Let us imagine, too, that it stands on an island in the middle of a lake, a fact which will preserve its remoteness. Around the lake is the forest or extensive park famous for its deer. There are long rides shaded by trees; there are rocks and grottoes and temples, foresters' cottages, statuary and ancient ruins carefully sited to enhance the landscape and to provide venues and romantic resorts suitable for the composition of poems or for the study of philosophy. In this forest there will be an atmosphere of quietness—deep shadows will be heightened by shafts of sunlight through the leaves making pools of light on the ground. This is the haunt of Satyrs. We are reminded of the forest of Fontainebleau and the park of Versailles, though all the time we will be closely in touch with the wooded parks of Warwickshire.

Part I. This scene is laid in the most civilized part of the park, where masonry in the form of temples and statues is placed to provide good vistas from the palace gardens. In the background we see across the lake the palace with its 'curious knotted garden'. On one side of the stage are steps cut out of the green turf and guarded by the statue of a stag, which is a chaste emblem of the King of Navarre. These steps form the boundary between the forest and the private purlieus of the King; probably the edict forbidding females to enter is placed at the foot of them, but at all events it is most important to plant the boundary line in our minds. When the play opens the King and courtiers are using this area as a pleasant, shady place to pursue their studies. After the disappearance of the court (Act I, Sc. 1) Don Armado and Moth land here from a boat in which they have been fishing (Act I, Sc. 2) and later on the Princess and her embassy wait at this point for the King to receive them (Act II, Sc. 1).

Part II. The second scene is laid deeper in the park where the scenery is more rustic. We can still see the lake in the background, though here it is less formal and more overgrown with rushes and sedge—a sort of backwater. On one side of the stage there is a forester's cottage. This cottage is in a romantic state of disrepair; it is the home of Don Armado which he uses also as a prison for Costard. It has a little balcony approached by a flight of steps, on which Berowne can sit 'like a demi-god in the sky' during the sonnet scene (Act IV, Sc. 3). The cottage is hung with remnants and trophies of the chase. On the opposite side the ground rises steeply so that we can visualize the 'steep up-rising of the hill' and all around this area the hunt takes place.

Part III. Here the Princess has erected her tent; the background of the lake and the palace are the same as in Part I. The tent creates a blaze of colour on one side of the stage. On the opposite side there is a natural stage which provides an impressive entrance for the Blackamoor-Russian procession and serves as the acting area for the Masque. At the end Mercade arrives in a great black barge in which the Princess and her ladies depart whilst, in the middle of the stage, lit by a lantern or two, the little group of rustics in their incongruous fancy dress, sing their song.

ANALYSIS OF THE CHARACTERS

The King of Navarre and his Court

Let us imagine Ferdinand of Navarre to be still in his twenties; a graceful, accomplished young monarch who has been strongly influenced by the new interest in learning and the classical cult of the Renaissance. Let us imagine, too, that he has lately succeeded his father, perhaps a traditionalist of the Old Tudor school. By contrast the young King is a modern Elizabethan. Like Hamlet he was born into a new world where religion, philosophy, science and politics were undergoing profound change and, like Hamlet, he sickens at the sycophants, parasites, duellists and yes-men of the old court life. Berowne's tirade against Boyet in Act V, Sc. 2 is reminiscent of Hamlet's jibes at Osric and suggests that Boyet and his ilk are the sort of courtiers on whom the new King and his companions have turned their backs.

In order to escape the out-moded atmosphere of the court Ferdinand has withdrawn to his summer palace, 'a little academe' where, together with his fellow humanists—Berowne, Dumain and Longavill—he purposes to follow the precepts of humanist philosophy. In principle we sympathize with their motives, but the youthful enthusiasm of these young men is not balanced by mature reason. They have pushed matters too far; confusing the truth of learning with the affectations of study. They are playing at being scholars and thoroughly enjoying their charade.

Their speech reflects such Renaissance affectations as:

> 'Taffeta phrases, silken terms precise,
> Three-piled hyperboles, spruce affectations,
> Figures pedantical . . .'

Their dress is a revolt against the rich costumes associated with kings and courtiers of tradition. In sartorial matters we must imagine they have inaugurated a sort of dress reform, expressive of their break with the past. In fact, though they mock the old affectations of exaggerated compliments and courtesies,

practised by the hand-kissing, lisping 'water-fly' Boyet, they
have themselves swung the pendulum so far in the opposite
direction that their own affectations are just as laughable. Their
excuse is that they are very young and for this we must finally
forgive them; for young fools are always forgivable in Shakespeare's eyes, but old fools never.

Our hearts warm to them at once when we see them in the
presence of the Princess and her ladies. Their revolutionary
principles, so brave when used to outrage some old blimps at
the court of Navarre, make them horribly uncomfortable when
exposed to the mocking eyes of the Princess, Rosaline, Maria
and Katherine. At each encounter, without daring to break
their oath of chaste monasticism, they make pathetic efforts to
attract their ladies' notice by sprucing themselves up with a
ribbon or a feather that can hastily be removed if misfortune
should cause one devotee of celibacy to meet another round
a corner. In the presence of death, or reality, at the end of the
play their theories are blown away like the gossamer of dande-
lions. We suddenly feel that these young men have grown up.
Like the youthful affectations of modern undergraduates, the
conceits of these make-belief academicians, their theories of
celibacy and their mock love-making and all the summer
fantasies of the 'little academe' are put back into time's play-
box to be taken out as generation succeeds generation—as
May-week and College balls, Freudian societies and poetry
readings on the Isis, velvet waistcoats and Oxford slang, have
taken their place, too, in the ancient receptacles of adolescence.

Shakespeare has not indicated much difference in character
between Ferdinand, Longavill and Dumain. All three are very
pleased with themselves, but by no means sure of themselves,
which excuses their priggishness. All three are affected in manner,
dress and language. They are obviously of much the same age
and have been close companions for many years. The King,
whilst adopting all the principles of equality with his fellows,
must have some slight ornament or chain, which distinguishes
him from them, and no doubt his dress is slightly richer
in its material, but differentiation of character must be mainly
left to the actors' personalities. If the play was written as a

masque for some country house festivity, it may be that the parts of these gallants and their ladies were intended for the host and his entourage, whilst the professional actors played the parts of the clowns. This would explain the lack of distinctive characterization which was beyond the histrionic powers of the aristocratic amateurs, but was inherent in their personalities. From our point of view these parts should be accepted as a challenge to personality, the actors' task being to impersonate young men of breeding, enjoying their game of playing scholars, revelling in the sound of high-flown words and in their ability to match their wit against each other in rapid 'sets', not unlike a set of tennis or the wise-cracking of American college boys. But pride must have its fall and Ferdinand, Longavill, Dumain and Berowne must come tumbling down with puppyish attempts to save their dignity. Such precipitations, from Malvolio's misfortunes to the clown who slips on a banana skin, invariably arouse the keenest amusement in an audience. It will be our task to play these parts in such a way that comedy can take its natural course and with such grace that priggishness is not advanced too far for sympathy to be endangered.

The Princess and her Ladies

As in all nicely balanced comedies the ladies are far more sensible than the gentlemen. We must imagine the Princess to be a charming, witty but responsible young lady. How otherwise would she be entrusted by her father with a difficult diplomatic mission? The ailing French King has reasoned that a charming young lady is more likely to get her way with a susceptible bachelor than a crusty old courtier. At the same time the young ambassadress must have her head well screwed on, lest she herself fall a victim to the charms of these bachelors and lose her suit. She has chosen as her attendants three young ladies no less charming than herself, though lacking her sense of responsibility. The party is accompanied, no doubt on the King's instructions, by an astute and experienced diplomat, of whom we shall have a word to say later.

Like the scholars of the court of Navarre, these maidens of

France are accomplished players of the Elizabethan game of wit; indeed they are better at it than the gentlemen and, being less engaged, emerge the victors. It is an exciting game and, as the success of their embassy largely depends on their ability to win it, they go to it with a will, generalled by the Princess and guided towards the weak chinks in their opponents' armour by the 'old love-monger' Boyet. All males are fair game to these ladies and when they have done with the scholars, they turn their wit against Boyet, who acts as their sparring partner and keeps them in training.

The Princess shows more signs of character than either Katherine or Maria, who like their lovers must be invested with personality by the artists who play them. We should note, however, that of these two, Maria is the youngest and, perhaps, the favourite of the Princess, whilst Katherine is the sparring partner of Rosaline, though she is easily hurt by Rosaline's unbridled tongue. The Princess has the makings of a capable and fascinating queen; she knows just when to play with her friends and when to command their respect; she can be serious and witty, but she is always conscious of her royal birth. She is more mature than the King of Navarre, but she is not lacking in sensitivity; her grief at the news of her father's death must come as no unnatural jolt to our reading of her character. But, if Rosaline, Maria and Katherine are less serious-minded than their mistress, we never feel that their hearts are proof against cupid's arrows. Despite their spirited powers of attack on the affectations of their suitors, their defences against love-making are but human, and the very ardour of their raillery betrays their inherent frailty. Had they been attacked by their suitors sincerely, individually and out of earshot of their companions, we would have seen how easily they could have been vanquished.

As it is, their defences fall before a cruel stroke of fate: the news of the death of the King of France causes the scene to cloud and things which hitherto were lightly regarded have suddenly to be seriously considered. The time for 'courtship, pleasant jest and courtesy' is over and the young ladies, who have attacked so successfully, are forced to confess their love.

Though their surrender is not ignoble, their common sense dictates a bargain with their lovers. Like sensibly bred young ladies, they demand that surrender shall only be made if honourable conditions are fulfilled and if the young gentlemen, by a twelvemonth's penance, prove themselves worthy of their victory.

Berowne and Rosaline

Of Rosaline we know that her wit is quicker, her tongue sharper, and her eye brighter than her playmates. She is 'the whitely wanton with the velvet brow'; her hair and eyes are black; she is provocative and enticing, flashing like a firefly in and out of the 'sets' of wit, stinging and jibing and capping the puns. She must be dressed to catch the eye, but not to occupy it with calm beauty as does her mistress. All these young ladies must be dressed with subtlety; their costumes must not be crude, yet they must radiate colour like butter-flies, catching the shafts of sunlight with startling glow and settling in the shade of the leaves without provoking attention. Rosaline is the dark lady of the Sonnets; the living embodiment of that provocative beauty who caught the gaze of a young man fresh from the fields of Stratford-upon-Avon, for whom he poured out so much of his youthful genius, not only in this play but also in his Sonnets, and as a result of whose whims he seems to have suffered so deeply.

As a complement to the Rosaline-Dark Lady portrait, Berowne seems to be like the young Shakespeare as we picture him in his early Sonnets and, indeed, with the exception of Prospero, this is the most subjective portrait that Shakespeare drew. Berowne has committed himself by word and by letter to the scholarly principles of his companions, but he has not accepted them in his heart. Unlike his companions, he prides himself on being a realist. His philosophy is empirical rather than ideological. He enjoys eating and flirting and revelling half the night as his fancy chooses. He believes that more things can be learnt by looking around him than by pouring over books; he is typically English in his dislike of new fashions or unseasonable preferences:

'At Christmas I no more desire a rose
Than wish a snow in May's new fangled shows;
But like of each thing that in Season grows.'

He considers that philosophy and astronomy are all right in their place, but all wrong out of it. Celibacy is to him contrary to the laws of nature and, therefore, impractical. All extremes are bad, and hard and fast rules are bound to be broken. In this Berowne shows himself as the pillar of sound English common sense, but, alas, he has his failings; he is just a bit too sure of himself. If others can accept the new decrees, so can he; he has no intention of being out-done in anything. What is more he can keep his oath, no matter what havoc temptation may wreak amongst his fellows. Like Benedict in *Much Ado* he makes the fatal mistake of considering himself stronger than young Master Cupid. Whatever tumbles Ferdinand, Dumain and Longavill may take as a result of their youthful conceits, no one falls harder or more comically than Berowne. He is not only more sure of himself than they, he is, like all good Englishmen, a true-born hypocrite. He has no intention of betraying his weakness to his fellows and every intention of mocking them for the beam that is firmly embedded in his own eye. For this fault we, as honest hypocrites, forgive him and enjoy it all the more when he is unmasked.

Berowne is very much the leader of the young scholars of Navarre and, although they are infuriated by his self-assurance, it is to him they turn for advice when they discover they are all foresworn. His wit extricates them from their broken promises and shows them a course of conduct. He becomes their natural leader when the 'sets' of wit with the girls take place; he overrules the King's fears of the effect of the masque on the ladies. Yet the actor must balance his blustering leadership with a modest sense of deference to the King, for if Berowne becomes too much of a bully, he loses our sympathy. To maintain this balance the actor must provide a special quality from within himself. We can best describe this by stating that he must be capable of exuding a mercurial warmth together with a sense of mischief and a sense of humour, and

18

never, never must he take himself too seriously for too long.

Don Armado and Moth

If Berowne be a model for Benedict, then perhaps we can say that Armado is a model for Malvolio, yet both Armado and Berowne stand in their own right as characters. Armado is a gentleman of fallen fortunes. This is important and places him on a higher shelf than the steward Malvolio. Armado is a sort of Don Quixote. Whether Shakespeare knew of Cervantes' immortal character or not is not important, for ideas once in the air come to roost in various pigeon-cots. Shakespeare through Don Armado expresses his own idea of the romantic Spanish knight-errant, who lives in an imaginery world of past grandeur, mistaking a peasant girl for a princess and bandying words instead of blows.

Don Armado, we must imagine, has wandered across the Pyrenees into Navarre in search of adventure and of a patron who will give him food and shelter, for he is very much out at elbows and cannot agree to fight in his shirt as he does not possess one. So he stumbles upon the 'little academe', where words are parried instead of sword thrusts. This cultural paradise suits him well, for he is a 'plume of feathers' in all matters relating to phraseology and has 'a mint of phrases in his brain'. He is not, of course, taken seriously by the young scholars, but used as an 'interim' for their studies and a butt for their recreation. Don Adriano de Armado, as he likes to be called, has his head too high in the clouds to see himself as others see him. Upon all he must confer his patronage with the air of a Spanish grandee. He bestows upon Costard the remuneration of three farthings with princely largess and, when with gross injustice he is accused of getting Jaquenetta with child, he must earn our undying respect by the magnificent condescension with which he offers to right her very tarnished honour. We must make sure that, in his ludicrous disguise as Hector, the blue blood of the Armados is plainly visible and, when he unbends to retort to the impudences of Moth, he must do so with due measure and decorum.

As for Moth, we must make sure he is in tune with his

master; little he may be, but pretty he is not. The part must be played by a boy not a girl, for Moth is no dolled up page-boy of nineteenth-century tradition, complete with snow-white hose and ill-disguised bosom. Quick witted he must be, for we cannot imagine how else the dignified Armado gets his daily bread; capable of taking a purse in a crowded street, glib of tongue, a slippery little eel to catch; impertinent to his master whose gravity of deportment he delights to imitate; knowing full well that the vain old gentleman will never realize to what extent he is being fooled. All this may be a pro-ducer's fancy, but we have no way of representing the satire that was intended by this character. The best we can do is create a living character in tune with the impertinence of the part.

Boyet

We have already said of Boyet that he is both an astute diplomatist attached to the Princess's mission and, also, the type of courtier against whom Ferdinand and his companions have turned their backs. We will present him as a middle-aged sycophant; an adept at the sort of raillery used by elderly Don Juans. His speech is affected; his gait and manner the product of the school of over-mannered yes-men who smirk and flatter themselves into their master's favour—a type which Shakespeare seems to have held in peculiar abhorrence. Twice in the play Berowne, as spokesman for his companions, draws a clear if rather cruel portrait of Boyet:

> 'This fellow pecks up wit as pigeon's peas,
> And utters it again when God doth please;
> He is wit's pedlar and retails his wares
> At wakes and wassails, meetings, markets, fairs . . .'
> 'A can carve too, and lisp; why this is he
> That kiss'd his hand away in courtesy . . .'
> 'This is the flower that smiles on everyone
> To show his teeth as white as whale's bone:
> And consciences, that will not die in debt,
> Pay him the due of "honey-tongued" Boyet.'

and again:

> 'Some carry-tale, some please-man, some slight zany,
> Some mumble-news, some trencher-knight, some Dick,
> That smiles his cheek in years, and knows the trick
> To make my lady laugh . . .'

But we must remember that Berowne was suffering under a severe smart when he utters these words, for Boyet had been largely instrumental in spoiling the Muscovite Masque and there has been a look about him recently which suggested to the young scholars that, however much of a fool they might consider him, he appears to have seen something amusing about them. To serious-minded pioneers of a new and, of course, better way of life, such ridicule is highly offensive.

So despite Berowne's biting strictures, we must not think too ill of Boyet. Indeed, were we to do so we would weaken the case for the good sense and charm of the Princess, for why should she tolerate a creature who is no more than a syco-phantic flatterer. For all his faults, Boyet must have a quality that the King and his followers lack—a sense of humour. All his gallantries with the young ladies would be intolerable if we did not see Boyet laughing at himself and chuckling at their chaff of him. He is in fact an amusing, old sugar-daddy whom the King of France has wisely chosen as a travelling companion for his daughter. He must be dressed in the height of fashion with all the vanities of an age which has never been equalled for the richness of its embroidery, its satins and velvets, and the beauty of its cobweb lace.

Costard and Jaquenetta

Here are two figures who might have slipped straight out of any Elizabethan allegorical poem. Jaquenetta, the blowsy, tumble-in-the-hay type of wench, and Costard, the rather nondescript yokel. Costard must not be presented as a court clown, like Feste, Touchstone or the Fool in *Lear*; he is the yokel clown—a slightly deformed creature, the product of the inbreeding of country villages. His dress must be colourful, but slovenly, with no hint of the cap and bells of Gilbert and

Sullivan's creation. Both he and Jaquenetta share the traditional cunning of the peasantry, the culmination of which is the foistering of Jaquenetta and her bastard upon the innocent Don Armado. Despite his villainy, Costard is a likeable creature with a delightful sense of mimicry, a simple sense of fun, and must show not a little amazement at the peculiar goings-on of his intellectual betters. We must take him readily to our hearts in the final masque when he feels a professional sense of shame in that bad fluff of 'big' for 'great'.

Dull, the Constable

Dull is a first sketch for Dogberry, though he gets little chance to show the immense, if ponderous, mental activity of that king of provincial officialdom. He is, as his name implies, remarkably dull in his wits; the whole aim of which are directed to the question of snatching a nice, little snooze. We feel that he has an enormous capacity for sleep, which overcomes him at all times of the day and in any place whatsoever. Having delivered up Costard to justice, we should feel that he has completed an immense effort and immediately he settles down for a good snore, only to be rudely awakened when his name is called. He is dressed in country fashion with a staff or chain of office to signify his beadledom and he is, withal, a man of considerable girth as befits his high office. All the more remarkable, then, when suddenly he announces that he will make one in a dance, or, if necessary, play the tabor. It is as if, with the mention of the masque, some distant stirring from his past comes upon him and we must see the worthy fellow gambolling cumbersomely with Costard to the music of the tabor and the pipes.

Holofernes and Sir Nathaniel

Here are a pair of as foolish old pedants as one could wish to find in any Elizabethan provincial town. Holofernes and Sir Nathaniel are essentially a pair; to separate them would make each an intolerably tedious old fellow. Sir Nathaniel's parsonical bleatings are as necessary a counterpart to Holofernes's intolerable Latin, as Verges's piping is to Dogberry's bass. They have, of course, nothing to do with the court of Navarre; we imagine them living in the village near by. Hearing that the young King has set up a scholastic establishment at the castle, they are hanging around to see what they can pick up in the way of a job, or at any rate a favour from the young, aristocratic scholars.

Despite the ravages that time has wrought by depriving these characters of the humour of topical satire, they should still be able to amuse a modern audience. The crabbed old schoolmaster, savouring his mumbo-jumbo language, smacking his lips over the misquotation from Mantuanus, or revelling in his preposterous alliterative verses, is a figure of fun to everyone whose recollections of schooldays are not entirely past. The village curate is an old stage joke, and Sir Nathaniel should prove no exception to the rule that curates cause mirth. The actors of these parts must, however, be prepared to bring a considerable degree of originality to the humour, if they are to avoid somewhat stereotyped stage characters from which the stuffing has been removed by the passage of time. They must constantly bear in mind that their position in the play is to provoke our 'ridiculous smiling' and all means that are in character must be employed to his end.

The Forester and Mercade

There is little to be said about the characters of these two. The former is a good, blunt fellow who gets into deep water when he tries to please the Princess. Mercade must not attempt to characterize his part; he must be fully aware of his importance to the mood of the play. His appearance at the end and the grim words he speaks are the effects by which the magic of the last scene is set in motion. He must appear almost featureless, like death itself, and as he steps upon the stage a chill must be felt throughout the mirthful proceedings of the mock duel. His voice must command respect, whilst expressing sympathy for his mistress so suddenly bereft of a father. He is both the messenger of death and a foreboding of the end of a summer's day, for with his entry the scene begins to cloud: the colours fade from the lake and trees, and the first shiver of autumn is felt.

And so our play draws towards its end. The young people are growing up and learning the bitterness, as well as the sweets of youth; the responsibilities that crowd out the youthful jests; the sorrows that make the joys more true. And, as these brilliant young people disappear in the deepening shade of a summer night, we hear the last notes of the simple people's song—a song which was born in Stratford long ago—and the melancholy hoot of the owl.

POSTSCRIPT

No postscript to this production would be complete without a special tribute to the composer and designer. The music that Herbert Menges provided for us, especially the haunting melody which lingered in ever diminishing phrases as the mystery of night fell over the forest, seemed to us an expression of our feelings about this play and food for our inspiration. I cannot think of *Love's Labour's Lost* without it.

Berkeley Sutcliffe, the designer, turned for his inspiration to the miniatures of Nicholas Hillyard and Isaac Oliver, from which he developed the glowing colours of his exquisite designs. The last days of our rehearsals, when the players rehearsed in these superb costumes for the first time, were, however, a severe shock to us all. Not that we were unaware of what our costumes were to be, but because the play had assumed a freedom of movement and a youthful virility whilst we were rehearsing it in our working clothes, which seemed to be lost, or restricted, when the players were encased in whalebones and ruffs.

This is a situation which happens all too frequently in the production of costume plays, which should always be rehearsed from an early stage, if not in the costumes that are to be used, at least in the costume of the period. The producer will spend three or four weeks building up the synthesis of text, movement and characterization, and ignore the fact that to build up his part an actor must work through his external appearance, no less than through his mental approach; the two are inextricably woven in the creation of character. An actor dressed in an open-necked shirt and jeans will assume a type of gesture, stance and movement which are totally incompatible with doublet, hose and trunks, and his confidence, perhaps his most important asset, will suffer severely when he finds himself restricted in unfamiliar garments.

A week's try-out at the Pavilion Theatre, Bournemouth, ironed out these difficulties and by the time we came to London the players had grown into their costumes and had rediscovered their style.

The first night of this production was a terrifying affair. We were following a series of seasons which were without parallel in the history of the Old Vic: the departure of Sir Laurence Olivier, Sir Ralph Richardson and John Burrell from the directorship of the company had been universally regretted. Moreover, we were presenting a play which was unlikely to draw a vast public. Yet somehow its charm, its youth and its lyrical loveliness carried us through. I cannot remember any play which produced a happier atmosphere back-stage than this. The last movement of this comedy of youth, when the great barge with its black flag, bearing the sorrowful Princess and her ladies, moved slowly away to the accompaniment of the song of spring, the gradual darkness shrouding the silhouette of Don Armado, the falling of a leaf from the summer trees, produced a sense of reverence in us all as we stood around in the wings, waiting for those strange enigmatic words, so charged with emotion—

'The words of Mercury are harsh after the songs of Apollo. You that way: we, this way.'

An owl hooted and the curtain fell.

HAMLET

HAMLET
Old Vic Theatre Company
New Theatre. 2nd February 1950

CLAUDIUS, *King of Denmark*	MARK DIGNAM
GERTRUDE, *Queen of Denmark*	WANDA ROTHA
HAMLET	MICHAEL REDGRAVE
GHOST OF HAMLET'S FATHER	WILFRED WALTER
POLONIUS	WALTER HUDD
LAERTES	PETER COPLEY
OPHELIA	YVONNE MITCHELL
HORATIO	MICHAEL ALDRIDGE
OSRIC	PAUL ROGERS
ROSENCRANTZ	GORDON WHITING
GUILDENSTERN	LEO MCKERN
MARCELLUS ⎫ *Officers*	⎧ GEORGE BENSON
BERNARDO ⎭	⎩ NORMAN WELSH
FRANCISCO, *A Soldier*	RICHARD WALTER
PLAYER KING	JOHN VAN EYSSEN
PLAYER QUEEN	BRIAN SMITH
LUCIANUS AND FIRST PLAYER	PAUL ROGERS
FIRST GRAVE-DIGGER	GEORGE BENSON
SECOND GRAVE-DIGGER	GORDON WHITING
VOLTIMAND ⎫ *Ambassadors*	⎧ ROLF LEFEBVRE
CORNELIUS ⎭	⎩ WILLIAM EEDLE
FORTINBRAS, *Prince of Norway*	RICHARD WALTER
A CAPTAIN	NORMAN WELSH
A PRIEST	WILLIAM EEDLE
REYNALDO	LESLIE GLAZER

LORDS, LADIES, OFFICERS, SOLDIERS, SAILORS, MESSEN-
GERS, AND OTHER ATTENDANTS:
ROSALIND BOXALL, JANE WENHAM, DELIA WILLIAMS,
COLIN CAMPBELL, JAMES GROUT, MICHAEL HARDING,
ROLF LEFEBVRE, DAVID PEACOCK.

Scenery and Costumes designed by Laurence Irving.
Music composed by Herbert Megens.

28

'A speech of some dozen or sixteen lines'

The inserted speech in the play scene

[*Photograph: John Vickers, London*]

[Photograph: John Vickers, London

HAMLET: Michael Redgrave

[Photograph: John Vickers, London

The Polonius Family

LAERTES: Peter Copley   POLONIUS: Walter Hudd

OPHELIA: Yvonne Mitchell

HAMLET

Too much has been written about this play. Let us, there-fore, avoid moralizing and conjecturing about the psycholo-gical condition of Hamlet, the sexual condition of the Queen, the question of whether Polonius is an historical caricature or not, the Renaissance spook controversy that raged round the appearance of spirits from the dead, and the many other fascinating, but theatrically irrelevant, problems raised by this play. Let us treat *Hamlet* as a play; a play which contains all the elements of good theatre from the most majestic verse to the most exciting melodrama. Let us leave the professors to bury themselves in their theories, in which pursuit they can only too easily succeed in losing the essential truth. For the truth about *Hamlet* is that it is intended for the theatre, and although it may be of interest to the psycho-analyst to place the characters on the operating table, there to measure and label their motives and impulses, such a process, if carried too far, can land the producer and the actors in disaster. It is a great error to confuse the operating theatre with the acting theatre.

The play was aimed at one of the most popular tastes ex-hibited by Elizabethan audiences, the taste for so-called revenge drama, of which *The Spanish Tragedy* is the most outstanding example. This taste it completely succeeded in satisfying, if we are to judge from the many contemporary references to it and to such box office indications as have come down to us.

The fact that the author has inevitably woven into this

29

drama of revenge the most profound philosophy, instead of the somewhat banal clichés of his contemporaries in the same field, the fact that he has succeeded in making his principal character a being of flesh and blood, instead of a pasteboard figure, has undoubtedly insured its immortality beyond the reach of shifting popular fancy for this or that type of play, but these facts have not made *Hamlet* into a different type of play. It is and remains a revenge play—a play of excitement and of forceful action, a play which should grip our attention and hold us on the edges of our seats from beginning to end by the force and drive of its plot. It is this plot—this story of a man called on to revenge his father's death—that must never be lost sight of in *Hamlet*, however absorbed we may be by the many fine passages of verse or telling twists of character. I intend to make the telling of this story with its full dramatic clash of characters and its swift moving and exciting action the central theme of this production. This I believe to be the proper way of serving the author's intention.

Now let us turn to this story—to this clash of mighty opposites which creates the drama of *Hamlet*. But before doing so, I would like to say a word about the atmospheric background of the play; for this background is the play's frame, adding point and colour to the drama which is unfolded inside it.

The Background of Hamlet

You will remember that in *Love's Labour's Lost* we discovered the atmospheric background lay in the pastoral, summer setting, in which the falling of evening lent particular point to the ephemeral quality of youth. Very different is the background of *Hamlet*, and I consider that insufficient attention has been paid in the past to what this background is. The superficial observer, influenced by the romantic criticism of the early nineteenth century or by the 'Sturm und Drang' influence of German productions, is apt to stress too heavily the theme of the gloomy Dane and impose upon the play the dark and dank atmosphere of a vast castle, in which the festering evils of Claudius's court flourish like a poisoned fungus. The young prince is seen against this background as a pale prisoner driven to the brink of madness by his struggle with his own romantic and vacillating nature. Some truth there is in this prison-like background, for to Hamlet's mind Denmark is a prison and the recent marriage of his mother to his uncle has soured his outlook. But the play is not a subjective piece of romanticism, in which the emphasis is laid on the ego of Hamlet. It is not, in my view, correct to see the play through Hamlet's eyes; this is the romantic and not the Elizabethan way of looking at life. Shakespeare has borrowed his plot from Elsinore and he is not forgetful of the peculiarities of this locality.

The castle of Elsinore stands on the sea—not on the high cliffs of a romantic seascape, but on the flat, monotonous coast of Denmark. It is a land of sand-dunes and estuaries, as well as of a busy sea trade, and is inhabited by a sailor race. Therefore, besides the castle itself which has, of course, a prison-like feeling about it to Hamlet, we have other possibilities of atmospheric background. We have the long, lonely estuaries in which, at low tide, ships lie on their sides like stranded sea-monsters; we have the call of sea-birds and the distant tolling of the bell-buoys; we have sea mists that add a feeling of lost-ness—of aloneness—to the countryside; we have the swelling full tides on which the boats ride proudly at anchor; we have the busy export trade and the naval dockyards of a country which, at that time, was rich and powerful and to whom both England and Norway were tributary kingdoms. All this may be geographically and historically true and even atmospheri-cally interesting, but is it intended or suggested by the author?

I believe it is. I believe Shakespeare gives as much indication of it as he can without the help of actual scenic aid. Let us look at the facts of the text. In the first scene we hear of shipwrights at work; in the second Voltimand and Cornelius are dispatched to Norway obviously by sea; in the third Laertes is about to go aboard and the ship is only a few minutes away from where he stands; in the sixth Reynaldo is about to embark in the wake of Laertes; in the seventh Voltimand and Cornelius have just returned from Norway. Then Hamlet is sent by sea to England and Fortinbras has just landed with his army to march through Denmark. Later we hear of pirates and a sea fight, and it is sailors who carry Hamlet's letter to Horatio. To my mind there is no doubt that Shakespeare was very conscious of this sea background; and whether or not the legend of Shakespeare's visit to Elsinore be true, it is clear that he set his play by the sea and was conscious of its influence on the action and atmosphere of the plot.

So I intend to make use of the sea atmosphere in this production of *Hamlet* and to place the whole play—the castle, the platform, the graveyard and the Fortinbras scene, on the very brink of it. This setting will, I believe, help us to understand the background of the late warrior King whose power depended on his command of the Straits of Elsinore, and the new ambitious King Claudius, whose power depends on diplomacy and treaties with his sea-faring neighbours. It will heighten the aloneness of Hamlet, portrayed against the solitary flat country of the Baltic coast, covered for a great part of the year by the mists that curl up from the sea, revealing cattle and houses like lost toys floating in its eddies and swirls. In such a land death takes its toll and the Royal House of Denmark is fated to yield up its harvest, as well as the simple fishermen and sailors who lie rotting in the graveyard on the sand-dunes.

So much for the atmosphere. Now let us turn to the protagonists of this drama of revenge.

Claudius

The kingdom of Denmark, so rich and powerful under the late King, has passed its peak and is in danger of losing its prestige as a naval power. Its tributary kingdom, Norway, is no longer easily held in submission now that Claudius, instead of his warrior brother, wears the crown. Youth, in the person of young Fortinbras, has begun to rebel. But Claudius, if no soldier himself, is no puppet King; he is capable and ambitious. He is one of those persons who lives for power and who knows that he has the ability to rule—to rule, but not to lead. He does not inspire confidence or affection, as we imagine his brother did. He rules by bullying, by bribes, by cunning, and by flattery. He knows precisely what effect flattery can have on Gertrude and Polonius. He is bland and good-humoured in outward behaviour; he knows how to impress Laertes with his bluffness, how to drink with his ambassadors, how to impress those susceptible to royal favour with an attitude of hail-fellow-well-met. All these qualities would make Claudius a successful and respected, if not exactly a much loved, King. His weakness is the heavy burthen that lashes his conscience— a brother's murder. Try as he may, he cannot overcome the lurking fear of the criminal—the fear of being found out. Like many bullies, he is, in emergencies, a coward and a sentimentalist about himself. He whines to Gertrude about his heavy load of troubles; he blubbers to the Almighty for assistance; he is reduced to a state of near panic after the play scene, and he hides behind Laertes in his plot to kill Hamlet. Above all, he is bitterly jealous of Hamlet, because he knows his nephew has inherited from his brother the natural good-will and leadership which he, Claudius, lacks. But his reign will not be an age of complete disintegration; if Claudius lacks prestige as a military leader, he will make use of power politics and diplomatic manœuvres to uphold his position. His opponents will score no easy victory over him. He will suppress the spirit of revolt and of liberalism which is budding in the persons of Fortinbras, Hamlet and Horatio with a heavy hand. A hand only covered with the velvet glove, because Claudius does not believe in showing his true colours until the right moment arrives. Moreover, his cruel nature is momentarily curbed by the influence of the Queen. It is this influence, the result of his guilty relationship with Gertrude, which causes his downfall. It is the Queen who restrains him from taking swift action upon Hamlet, though he knows well the latter is a danger to his hold on the throne. The major dramatic clash of the play, then, is between the characters of Claudius and Hamlet. These two have nothing in common with each other; the one hard-fisted, shrewd and unscrupulous, glib of tongue, affecting bluffness and good nature; the other—and here we have to pause to consider what are the main characteristics of Claudius's opponent.

Hamlet

Hamlet, we have said, is not a gloomy Dane, nor is he a man

who could not make up his mind. The facts deny these two conceptions. First, for the gloom: there is hardly a character in the whole calendar of heroic and tragic drama who displays more humour than Hamlet. Nor is this humour solely of the sarcastic variety displayed in his encounters with Polonius, Rosencrantz, Guildenstern and Osric; with Horatio and the players Hamlet displays a gentle humour untinged by sarcasm. Next, for the theory that he is unable to make up his mind. Hamlet is informed by a ghost that his father has been murdered by his uncle. This murderer has now married his mother. He is bidden to revenge this fearful act. The first point is that this message is conveyed to him by a spirit from another world and to the Elizabethans there was grave doubt about the nature of such apparitions. They were either, like Horatio, inclined to disbelieve in them, or, if they were actually confronted by an apparition, they considered it to be an evil spirit sent to lead them astray. This is Hamlet's dilemma—'the spirit that I have seen may be the devil'—and it is a dilemma which any contemporary man of Hamlet's age, or indeed of our own, would find equally perplexing. He must prove the good faith of the ghost. He chafes at his own delay, he considers himself to be a 'dull and muddy-mettled rascal' who 'peaks, like John-a-dreams, unpregnant of his cause', but he is being unjust to himself, and we must not, as some certain others have done, take him too literally.

Having once proved the veracity of the ghost by the effect of the ghost's story upon the King in the play scene, Hamlet does not delay an instant in making up his mind. Hardly more than a few minutes after the end of the play, he is about to plunge his sword into the King's back as he prays, from which act he is only restrained by the feeling that such a death is too good for this murderer:

> 'Now might I do it pat, now he is praying;
> And now I'll do it: and so he goes to heaven:
> And so am I revenged? That would be scanned;
> A villain kills my father; and for that,
> I, his sole son, do this same villain send

34

To Heaven.
O, this is hire and salary, not revenge.
He took my father grossly, full of bread,
With all his crimes broad blown, as flush as May;
. . . and am I then revenged,
To take him in the purging of his soul,
When he is fit and seasoned for his passage?
No . . .'

I would ask you to note the repetition of the word revenge
in this soliloquy. This, as I have said, is a revenge play and it
behoves the revenger to accomplish his task in the proper
manner. Revenge has its etiquette, and it would not do at all
for Hamlet to kill the King, if the victim is unaware of the
motive behind his death. It is this desire for just revenge,
rather than vacillation of purpose, which holds Hamlet from
the accomplishment of his mission.

A few minutes after this temptation to kill the King, he sees
a better opportunity and runs his sword through a curtain
behind which he believes the King to be hiding. I see no uncertainty of purpose in either of these incidents. The fact that
he kills not the King but Polonius, is a severe blow to him;
it delays his act of revenge and makes him despair of ever
accomplishing his mission. He tortures himself with this
further delay, calling it 'bestial oblivion' and a 'craven scruple',
but is it? The facts say no; and after all it is only natural for
Hamlet to feel thwarted, to blame himself for failing to
accomplish his mission. Again and again in this play I find we
must avoid the romantic view of seeing the play through
Hamlet's eyes. We must not believe everything Hamlet says
about himself; we must regard him as a man with a mission
for revenge who tortures himself because fate, rather than his
own nature, does not deliver the victim to him easily.

No sooner is Hamlet on the sea than he manages with great
determination to throw off his guards; again no uncertainty of
purpose. Having done so, he returns to accomplish his task
without delay. There is no evidence, other than Hamlet's
own natural feeling of frustration, to support the claim that

this prince is infirm of purpose or unable to make up his mind.

Having laid aside these two popular illusions about Hamlet, let us turn to what I believe him to be. He is not an epic figure like Macbeth or Timon or Lear, by which I mean he is not an outsize personality who creates the drama round him. Hamlet is a normal man, albeit a prince, set against an epic situation. When I say normal I do not mean that he is not a very gifted person; that he is not a philosopher, a poet and an advanced thinker; that he is not emotional and sensitive. I mean he is a human being and not a type of superman who suffers from an advanced condition of egomania. Hamlet is neither puffed up with pride, nor over-ambitious; he is not lustful, mad nor greedy. He represents both what we would all like to be, and in some ways what we all are. He loves simple people, like Horatio and the players. He is attached to his mother and horrified at her over-hasty wedding. He is a good companion and obviously liked by such simple people as Bernardo and Marcellus. He is much attached to Ophelia and infuriated that she should be a party to the conspiracy against him. He recognizes the good in the soldierly qualities of Fortinbras and his captain. He dislikes sycophants, like Osric, tedious old schemers, like Polonius, and above all he dislikes Claudius. Even if Claudius and Hamlet were not destined to be so inextricably bound up together, they would have hated each other, for they are, as Hamlet says, mighty opposites. The one is a man to whom justice is all important, the other is a man who has no scruples in riding over it. There is nothing outsize about Hamlet. If he is driven to extremes by his mission, if he is tortured by his mother's shame, if he is infuriated by Ophelia's treachery, if he is unmoved by the deaths of Polonius, Rosencrantz and Guildenstern, if in his despair he is even driven to contemplate suicide, we still have no reason to consider his reactions to all these events as an indication of melancholia, or Oedipus-complex, or instability of mind, or anything other than the natural reactions of a man such as you or I when placed in a like dilemma.

That I believe to be the truth about Hamlet, and the reason for the popularity of his character with the audience. If the actor of Hamlet fails to touch the heart, the reason must lie in his failure to touch the common sentiment of our own experience. Hamlet is a man beset by trials of an almost insupportable magnitude, and, when he comes triumphantly through them, our love goes out to him as to a human being. Then we can say, as our hearts swell with pride at the nobility and greatness of man,

> '. . . good-night, sweet prince,
> And flights of angels sing thee to thy rest.'

The clash between Hamlet and Claudius is, as we have said, the main dramatic theme of the play. Let us now consider the rest of the characters who are built up around this clash, heightening its tension and pointing its significance.

The Ghost

The ghost is the machinery of the play without whom the clash would never have occurred. He lays upon Hamlet this fearful mission of revenge and complicates it by enjoining him to contrive nothing against his mother; although he has said enough about Gertrude to rouse Hamlet's full fury against her. The ghost of the late King Hamlet must prevent a complete contrast to Claudius. He is the great warrior King—the embodiment of chivalry. It is a difficult part to play, which is perhaps why Shakespeare played it himself, for the ghost must strike a note of genuine awe and terror. If the actor fails to make us believe in the ghost the whole fabric of the drama is endangered. This must have been no easy task on a platform in an open courtyard without the aid of artificial lighting. It is no easy task to-day when all the aid of stage machinery can only too easily make the ghost even more ridiculous.

Horatio

Horatio presents no major problem for the actor endowed with the right personality, but it is not a foolproof part like Kent in *Lear*. Horatio has little to say, but his presence is always important. He is a true friend, but by no means a cypher to Hamlet. He knows more than he is told, for he is sensitive to people's moods and not slow at putting things together. We notice that he talks most when away from Hamlet, and in his presence his remarks are mostly confined to short sentences which are very much to the point and devoid of elaboration. This is an important basis of his relationship with Hamlet with whom words are not important, but who is for him always his Prince as well as his friend. He is the only mortal in the play, beside Hamlet, who knows the whole truth, but he realizes that this is a problem which Hamlet can only solve for himself; advice from him would be useless. So he suffers for Hamlet and with Hamlet and can do no more for him than render the creature comforts of clothing him when he is naked and supporting him when he dies. Yet the real comfort Horatio brings to Hamlet is his warmth, his silent sympathy, his genuine and simple love—a love so great that he is ready to die with his Prince. So I say this part presents no major problem to the actor, providing he is able to show that warmth and present that simplicity. He must be able to act an uncomplicated rock of steadfast loyalty which Hamlet describes 'as just a man as e'er my conversation coped withall'.

Polonius and his Family

Laertes is the opposite of Horatio; for whereas Horatio is unselfish and unostentatious, we have reason to believe that Laertes is neither. But Laertes must be considered in relationship to the Polonius family group; for, as so often in Shakespeare, we find here a little family group conceived as a family rather than as unrelated individuals. Such family groupings are found in the Capulet and Hotspur families, and elsewhere. There is in this Shakespeare family grouping an interesting study for the professors to pursue, if only they would not push their studies too far and realize that they are dealing with plays for the stage, and not subjects for the laboratory.

But there is no doubt that we can understand both Laertes and Ophelia better, if we realize that the author has conceived them as the children of Polonius; so let us first look at the father before we turn to the children.

Polonius is not a buffoon, as he was often portrayed in the

eighteenth century, nor is he a dear old man, as he is sometimes played to-day. He is a statesman in his decline—a conservative clinging to the old order, unable to change his views although quite willing to change his allegiance. He is the ageing civil servant, loyal to the crown, which for him is always right no matter how it has been won, applying his rather superficial knowledge of human character arbitrarily to all cases. His view is blinkered to a certain way of life and he cannot see beyond it, for he is old and has lost touch with life outside the council chamber. He is not an unkind father by intention, but proves to be so in practice. His use of Ophelia as a decoy to Hamlet shows considerable insensibility to his daughter's feelings. His advice to Laertes and to Ophelia is of the safety-first variety, which is quite satisfactory providing head rules heart and there are no extraneous complications. He is smug and satisfied with himself. He is a tyrant to his household, inclined to give banal views on life—a trait which Laertes in his advice to Ophelia has inherited. We must understand, too, that Polonius is beginning to enter the age of dotage. He constantly repeats himself, he is always losing the thread of his argument and many of his more banal remarks should not be regarded as a measure of his brain as it has been, but rather as the decline of a brain which may well have been a good one; a brain that is losing the ability to think things out afresh and falls back on clichés. But in order to have reached the position he has in the State, we must believe there is some truth in his question:

'Hath there been such a time—I'ld fain know that—
That I have positively said "'tis so",
When it proved otherwise?'

The tragedy of Polonius as a statesman is that he has just reached the time when it is going to prove otherwise rather too often. But he still holds his authority as a father and retains his position at court by being careful to tender such advice as may prove acceptable, or at least innocuous, to Claudius. Polonius is not a very likeable character. His dispatching of Reynaldo to trap his son, Laertes, in Paris, and his use of his daughter as a decoy to her lover is all part of his spying, mistrustful nature; and his habit of listening at keyholes brings him to the unexpected discovery of a sword through his guts. He did not, perhaps, deserve quite such a punishment, but in the clash of mighty opposites there is no quarter given.

The children are not replicas of the father, that would be untrue to the nature of families, but they are what they are largely because of him.

Laertes is a tough, captain-of-the-rugger team type of young man, inheriting from his father a glib way of advising others how to overcome their difficulties, as instanced in his advice to Ophelia. He has inherited, too, something of his father's dishonest nature by accepting too easily the King's ruse for killing Hamlet with a poisoned sword. The fact that he does this under emotional stress and repents his action almost before he has performed it, does not excuse him in our eyes. Like his father he is not completely dishonest, but chooses impulsively the dishonest path. His impulsive nature, as instanced by his hastily organized revolution against the King, his precipitate behaviour in the graveyard both to the priest and to Hamlet and his acceptance of the King's murderous proposal, displays a considerable streak of rashness in his character which is, as far as the play is concerned, his predominant feature. We have reason to believe that rashness was one of Polonius's characteristics also. But, because the father was a statesman, it did not take quite so brazen a form as it does in the sportsman son. Was it not rashness, however, for the old man to plant himself behind the arras in the Queen's bedroom? How did he imagine he could explain it away if Hamlet had uncovered him? In fact the final epitaph for him and his son seems to be:

'Thou wretched, rash, intruding fool, farewell.'

The redeeming feature of the Polonius family is their underlying affection for each other, and their sense of family honour. Despite Laertes's sententious advice to his sister and despite Polonius's ill-considered injunctions to his daughter, there is real affection displayed between them. Laertes is clearly fond of Ophelia, as well as jealous of her honour. His deep grief at her madness and his wild fury at her death are sufficient proof. So, too, we see that Polonius shows a similar care for Ophelia's honour, and is never purposely unkind to her. The unifying feature, therefore, in their family life is Ophelia who, by her gentleness and love, welds the family together and brings out the best in father and son. Ophelia does not share the rashness inherent in the menfolk of her family; her fault is in being too compliant. We must not blame her too heavily for this. Obedience is a virtue and Ophelia only obeys under protest. When her father chides her for giving too much time to Hamlet's society, she shows considerable spirit in his and in her own defence, but this spirit is not strong enough to prevent her from ultimate compliance in affairs which she knows to be wrong.

Ophelia, unlike Laertes and Polonius, has a very acute sense of right and wrong, but her failure lies in her lack of confidence in herself, in her too great trust in her family. She gives way too readily, 'I will obey, my lord' is her death knell. Perhaps this is the fault of Polonius for being too much of a petty tyrant, or of Laertes for being too positive in his views. But no matter for this, it is through her fatal compliance that Ophelia loses Hamlet's love and it is the knowledge of her own failure, as well as of her father's death, that causes her madness. We must, of course, love Ophelia and forgive her for she is only a girl, placing too much trust in her male relatives, and unable to cope with the mighty forces at work. But as we look at her pityingly, we cannot help comparing her to Cordelia, no less a child, who would have coped very differently with the situation.

The Queen

The other member of the weaker sex, Gertrude, suffers like Ophelia from not being cast in the heroic mould. She, too, fails because she is not heroic enough to cope with the clash of mighty opposites. The tragedy of Gertrude and of Ophelia is that though both are in their own ways warm and affectionate people, they are unable to bring comfort or help to those they love and are cast away almost unwept in the struggle that rages round them. How a Volumnia, a Lady Macbeth, or a Constance would have stood up to this situation we cannot say, but Gertrude does not belong to this tribe of women, she is completely feminine. Her fault lies in her self-indulgence and in her fatal habit of closing her eyes to unpleasant facts. She is, however, by no means lacking in virtues and she is not a weakling. She has committed a fatal crime before the curtain rises—adultery with her brother-in-law. By concealing this love from her late husband and by protesting constant devotion to him she has deepened her sin. The circumstances of this deception do not matter, the play demands that we do not excuse her for it. We are bidden, however, to see the sort of woman she is. Gertrude is beginning to age, she is maybe thirty-eight or forty-eight, according to whether we believe Hamlet to be twenty or thirty—Shakespeare has been purposely misleading on this point as he is on all questions of time. The salient fact is that, whilst she is still desirable, she is afraid of losing her attraction. She is what we would call to-day a highly sexed woman, for whom sex is, if not a necessity, at all events a major theme of her existence. Therefore, to her happiness Claudius's love is vital. But she is also a mother who is devoted to her son, and she is a woman with a sense of right and wrong. Her fault lies in her deliberate sacrifice of her conscience in order to indulge her selfish and lustful desires.

We are given no hint as to whether Gertrude was an accomplice to, or knew the truth about, her husband's death. She may know the truth or she may only suspect the truth, we need not decide this ourselves for it is not essential to the action. What is important for us to portray is that she does not want to think about the truth. She is deliberately shutting her mind to what she knows or suspects, and her main desire is to blot out the past and to enjoy the present. She wants her new life to be happy. She wants Claudius to love her. She wants Hamlet to love her. She wants her husband and her son to be friends.

> 'Good Hamlet, cast thy nighted colour off,
> And let thine eye look like a friend on Denmark.'

Don't let us mourn too long—'all that lives must die'—let

us be happy in the present is her philosophy. Behind it all, behind her well-cared for exterior, there is a horrible lurking suspicion, or an actual soul-searing knowledge. But she believes she has the ability to live on the surface of life without troubling about the depths, and she wants everyone else to do the same. The difficulty about this is that Hamlet cannot live on the surface, and it is Hamlet who drags the truth in front of her, forcing her to face the thing which she wants to hide:

'. . . almost as bad, good mother,
As kill a king, and marry with his brother.'

'As kill a king!'—that one ejaculation brings the past flooding up in front of her, the horrible, inescapable truth, the truth she has tried so hard to forget. 'As kill a king!' 'Ay, lady, 'twas my word' . . . There is no escaping it, if Hamlet will not let it rest. She struggles vainly against her buried conscience:

'O, Hamlet, speak no more;
Thou turn'st mine eyes into my very soul . . .'

'O, speak to me no more;
These words like daggers enter in my ears,
No more, sweet Hamlet!' . . .

'No more'—she is exhausted by the fight with herself; by her attempts to avoid the mirror of her past which her son is holding up to her, as he confronts her with the two pictures of her husband and her husband's murderer.

After this fatal interview with Hamlet following the play, she knows she has got to face facts. I consider that in the acting of the Queen's part a clear change should be made in her attitude to Claudius from this scene onwards. Up to now she has been amorous. Now a certain coldness should be evident, even a slight repulsion which good form and a sense of loyalty will not allow her to make too obvious. She does not desert Claudius, but she can no longer return to her old surface existence. She will follow him to whatever end fate may hold in store for the two of them. She will defend him in the face of his enemies, but her love for him has dried up inside her. She can hardly bear to touch him. She can no longer comfort

43

him, when he feels the weight of his trouble and guilt. From now on she is Hamlet's mother and Queen of Denmark, but not Claudius's bedfellow. Claudius, too, should be aware of her change towards him. From now on he drives his own path towards the removal of Hamlet without reference to her or her feelings.

As a pathetic, though not a heroic figure, Gertrude dies. We can now see in retrospect that the ghost was right in his injunction to Hamlet:

> '. . . leave her to heaven,
> And to those thorns that in her bosom lodge
> To prick and sting her.'

For Gertrude has a conscience and, though it took much to waken it from its slumber, it led her finally along a truer path, even if there is no complete redemption for her earlier sins. She dies trying to save her son against the treachery of her husband:

> 'No, no, the drink, the drink—O my dear Hamlet
> The drink, the drink! I am poisoned.'

It is the only positive gesture she performs in the play.

And now let us turn from the kings and queens, the rooks and knights, and look at the pawns in this mighty game of chess. For much of the drama comes from the skilful manipulation of these important pieces. The King's pawns are Rosencrantz and Guildenstern; Hamlet's pawns are the players. We must notice what dramatic use the author has made of these pieces.

Rosencrantz and Guildenstern

First, the King produces his pawns—two fellow students of Hamlet. Because of their poverty he has found no difficulty in suborning these two gentlemen to his purposes. Hamlet is not slow in realizing the King's game. He finds himself ringed round with spies: Polonius, Ophelia, Rosencrantz and Guildenstern; his every movement watched, his every motive suspected. He feigns madness to cover his tracks. Ophelia's job is to test whether he is mad for love; Rosencrantz and Guildenstern's job is to assess to what extent ambition for the crown lies behind his strange behaviour. But they have small chance against Hamlet and at their first interview they show their hand in the most clumsy fashion. This is one of the most fascinating scenes in the play, with its subtle innuendoes and in its play of Hamlet's rising suspicion of the strange fencing of the two spies. Note how Rosencrantz leads the conversation to the subject of ambition. Hamlet declares that to him Denmark is a prison:

'ROSENCRANTZ: Why, then your ambition makes it one; 'tis too narrow for your mind.

HAMLET: O, God, I could be bounded in a nut-shell, and count myself a king of infinite space, were it not that I have bad dreams.'

A glance from Rosencrantz to Guildenstern—press him again, your turn this time:

'GUILDENSTERN: Which dreams indeed are ambition; for the very substance of the ambitious is merely the shadow of a dream.'

A bit far-fetched this: Hamlet shoots a quick glance at Guildenstern; what are they up to?

'HAMLET: (carefully choosing his words) A dream itself is but a shadow.

ROSENCRANTZ: (leading Hamlet back to the subject) Truly, and I hold ambition of so airy and light a quality that it is but a shadow's shadow.'

Hamlet's suspicions are aroused. What is this repetition of the word ambition? But for the moment he cannot penetrate their purpose. Are they commissioned to catch him out? It looks like it, but he must have proof. That proof is visual. He breaks up the conversation:

'HAMLET: Shall we to the court? for, by my fay, I cannot reason.

ROSENCRANTZ
and
GUILDENSTERN: We'll wait upon you.'

As the Prince, he goes first to the door, then he turns suddenly and at that moment catches the two whispering together. This may be imposed stage business, but who has the right to deny its legitimacy or indeed its authenticity? And then Hamlet is on to them, pressing the truth out of them:

> 'Were you not sent for? Is it your own inclining?
> Is it a free visitation? Come, deal justly with me:
> come, come; nay, speak.'

Angered by their failure and by Hamlet's contempt for them, Rosencrantz and Guildenstern reveal the true baseness of their characters by allowing themselves to be used as Hamlet's gaolers and lead him to his death in England. They deserve their fate for 'they did make love to their employment and are not near our conscience'. What sort of men are they?

We are not given much indication. We know them to be poor and presumably in the habit of taking up jobs during university vacations. Of the two Guildenstern seems more stupid than Rosencrantz, who on several occasions has to come to the rescue of his fellow conspirator when the latter gets too deeply embroiled. We know that university students were drawn from a very wide social field and these two are obviously far from being of noble birth. We can, I think, legitimately break away from the elegant young courtier types who are usually presented, and find prototypes among the less reputable students, often not above murder or theft, who were the student companions of such men as François Villon. We may legitimately imagine that Rosencrantz is the smarter of the two, or, if you prefer it, he is the more obvious 'spiv'—whereas Guildenstern is a useful but clumsy thug who follows him around, sometimes to Rosencrantz's acute embarrassment.

These, then, are the King's pawns, and no sooner has he advanced them than Hamlet, at a momentary loss for a return move, hears his pawns approaching—they are the players.

The Players

Unlike Rosencrantz and Guildenstern, the players are un-conscious of the role they are playing, but obviously there is something afoot when Hamlet inserts some dozen or sixteen lines into the play. The players don't ask questions about such things—it was better not to know too much about political matters, for it was not uncommon in Elizabethan times for great men to use plays for their own political purposes, *vide Richard II* and the Essex riots. The players are a fresh untainted wind which blows through the castle of Elsinore. They should bring with them not only their own cheerfulness and joy of living, but a welcome vision of the outside world, far distant from the lonely Danish castle. They are happy people; a little over-exuberant as is natural when they find that their old patron has not forgotten his past association with them. This exuberance is directed at Polonius, who is bent on putting them in their place, and draws on them a mild rebuke when Hamlet says to their leader 'and look you, mock him not'.

They are not a collection of ham actors, nor a tired touring company. They come from the city where they are the leading troupe, and we must allow them no less mastery of their trade than was possessed by Burbage and his fellow actors of the Globe. The first player, clearly the Burbage of the troupe, is given the task of speaking the inserted lines—these are the lines spoken by Lucianus, not by the Player King—and he does so with great effect, although there appears to be an awful moment at the beginning when his memory fails him and the excited Hamlet cries:

> 'Begin, murderer; pox, leave thy damnable faces,
> and begin.'

I like to think this is a lapse of memory on the part of the leading player—and what could be more natural when new lines are inserted into a familiar text—rather than a display of ham acting. Hamlet has already given his instructions about the style of acting he requires, and we must give the players credit for obeying his instructions. If these 'damnable faces' are in fact a dry on the part of Lucianus, when suddenly confronted with this new speech, it adds a telling dramatic point to the climax of the play and adds an awful pause in which Hamlet's suspense is acute.

Osric

The next pawn advanced by the King is Osric. He has no active part to play other than to tempt Hamlet to the duel. In this he succeeds in spite of himself; for it is not the account he gives of Laertes's prowess which provokes Hamlet to fight, but rather some premonition of the end of all his labours which draws Hamlet to try his skill with the rapier and to the conclusion of his mission.

> '. . . If it be now, 'tis not to come; if it be
> not to come, it will be now; if it be not now,
> yet it will come; the readiness is all.'

It is strange that such a waterfly, a please-man, sponging and scraping before the King, should be chosen as the messenger of death, and yet it is fine dramatic irony that he is so chosen. Osric is not effeminate; he is the typical courtier of the age— the sycophant, the clever swordsman, the time-server, the flatterer whom Shakespeare most disliked and most ridiculed in Boyet, for example, and in the fawning spaniel Oswald in *Lear*. It is a telling part, this messenger of death caparisoned in finery and a master of courtesies.

Francisco, Bernardo and Marcellus

There is no great character drawing here, nor should the actors attempt to over-characterize these parts. The purpose of the three soldiers is purely functional. They are to build up and sustain the atmosphere and tension of the ghost scenes. Shakespeare knew, as we know to-day, that a ghost on the stage was a dangerous device, liable to provoke mirth rather than horror. He chose his ghost's pawns carefully, casting them as honest, straightforward soldiers, who would be unlikely to be moved by spiritual manifestations. If such men accepted the presence of the ghost then it would help the audience to do so. It is perhaps a measure of Shakespeare's skill that the ghost scenes, the most dangerous situations in the play, are the best written from the atmospheric point of view, and these three parts, particularly Bernardo and Marcellus, are parts that no actor can fail to find rewarding.

Voltimand and Cornelius

Then there are the very minor parts of Voltimand and Cornelius; nobody's pawns in particular, but most necessary to the story. Their task is to keep alive the Fortinbras theme, so that it comes as no great shock to the development of the play. They must be of a worthy age and well skilled in diplomacy, for they have a delicate task to perform and they manage it with success.

The Grave-Diggers

By way of contrast these two other minor parts have plenty of character. Their purpose in the play is a dual one. Firstly, they must provide a welcome relief to the high pitched tension of the revenge theme, and by refreshing us with their comedy, build up our emotions for the mighty conclusion. So it is that their roles are slung between Ophelia's death and the full harvest which the 'fell serjeant' is yet to demand.

Their second purpose is to lead Hamlet towards the grave by making him face death as a practical fact, as something which everyone must come to, as the great leveller which respects neither poor Yorick, nor Alexander, and so prepare him for his own end. Hitherto Hamlet has seen death as 'the undiscovered country from whose bourn no traveller returns'; now here in the graveyard he sees the other side of death, as a matter of bones and skulls and as a question of how long a man may lie in the earth before he rots. It is a macabre picture and yet much of death's sting is softened and humanized by such a homely way of looking at it. The grave-diggers lead Hamlet to the contemplation of a thing which had up to now given him cause to pause, and they enable him to think less of 'what dreams may come when we have shuffled off this mortal coil'.

Fortinbras

Last of all comes Fortinbras. To him falls the all important task of cleansing the stage from the putrefaction of death, of opening the doors of this ill-fated castle to the health-giving rays of the sun, of raising our hopes for a future free from the corrupting evil of crime and so laying the ghost that haunts these battlements. On the entrance of Fortinbras and his army, death throws off its horror, and we rise to the heights of great tragedy which can make us so much greater than ourselves, as we see Hamlet, his great task of revenge accomplished, carried like a soldier to the stage.

POSTSCRIPT

In June 1950 we took this production to Elsinore and played it in the castle courtyard. The players arrived in the late afternoon from Zurich and after a lengthy Danish supper in the Marienlyst Hotel, they joined me in the castle for a rehearsal which we realized would have to be prolonged into the small hours.

All went smoothly until after midnight, when, the castle 'bell then beating one', we were surprised by the loud singing of a blackbird which in the strange stillness of those grey walls was peculiarly distracting. Smoking is strictly forbidden in the castle courtyard and we broke off to enjoy a cigarette on the grass rampart overlooking the sea. Our surprise was considerable when on emerging from the moonlit courtyard we saw the dawn breaking over the Swedish coast opposite us. It was a russet dawn; the sea was the colour of dried blood, and, stranger than all, the comparatively flat Swedish coastline assumed, by virtue of the rising sun, the appearance of 'yon high eastward hill'. Just then a cock crowed, and we knew how it was that Horatio and the watch observed the dawn so shortly after midnight—'the dawn with russet mantle clad' that frightened the ghost from the battlements. Perhaps the Danish belief that Shakespeare visited Elsinore is not so legendary after all; at all events the castle records establish that English actors played there on more than one occasion during Shakespeare's lifetime.

Looking back on this production, it is now clear to me that the method we used to create the atmosphere of *Hamlet* was impressive, but mistaken. Very few Shakespeare plays benefit from pictorial scenery and, although the picture-frame stage of our theatres cannot be changed into the platform stage of the Globe, some kind of compromise must be found between the illusionist scenery of the picture-frame and the neutral acting area of the platform.

The painted back-cloth, though it may have a value in telling the spectators where they are and what it looks like, robs them of the use of their imagination. Shakespeare wrote his plays in such a way that the audience—so long as it listened attentively—knew where it was. As to the question of what it looks like, each member of the audience was free to conjure up his own mental picture. In fact, it is only on rare occasions in *Hamlet* that the audience requires a picture of the scene and on those occasions the words provide the necessary stimulant to the imagination—

'The air bites shrewdly; it is very cold'—

'But look, the morn, in russet mantle clad,
Walks o'er the dew of yon high eastern hill'

The imagination is fired by these verbal stimulants, the mind conjures up a mental picture. Once we paint the scene on a back-cloth, these words become superfluous. The mind of the spectator ceases to function; we sit back and listen to the beautiful poetry, but the purpose of the poetry is lost.

Now, there is plenty for the spectator to assimilate in *Hamlet* without providing him with the additional burden of creating the scenery for himself. Yet the provision of elaborate scenery is more of a hindrance than an aid to the understanding of the play. The spectator is lost in wonder at the beauty of the setting; he is intrigued to know just how the ghost works, and, as a result, he becomes inattentive to the words. The greater the scope of a play, the simpler must be its scenery. Elaboration, however atmospheric, must be avoided. The producer of to-day is forced, because of the type of theatre in which he works, to provide some kind of pictorial setting. He must strive to achieve his effects by the simplest means, using the symbol, rather than the illusion, of reality.

When we acted *Hamlet* on a platform against the bare grey wall of Elsinore, it sprang to life as never before.

TWELFTH NIGHT

TWELFTH NIGHT
Old Vic Theatre Company
14th November 1950

ORSINO, *Duke of Illyria*	ALEC CLUNES
VALENTINE ⎱ *Gentlemen attending on*	⎰ JAMES GROUT
CURIO ⎰ *the Duke*	⎱ RICHARD PASCO
A SEA CAPTAIN	MARK DIGNAM
SIR TOBY BELCH	ROGER LIVESEY
SIR ANDREW AGUECHEEK	ROBERT EDDISON
FESTE	LEO MCKERN
MALVOLIO	PAUL ROGERS
SEBASTIAN	PIERRE LEFEVRE
ANTONIO	WILLIAM DEVLIN
FABIAN	PAUL HANSARD
A PRIEST	ANTHONY VAN BRIDGE
VIOLA	PEGGY ASHCROFT
MARIA	PAULINE JAMESON
OLIVIA	URSULA JEANS
PAGE	DOROTHY TUTIN

SAILORS, LORDS AND OFFICERS:
ANTHONY VAN BRIDGE, RUPERT DAVIES, PETER DUGUID, PAUL HANSARD, RICHARD WALTER.

LADIES ATTENDING OLIVIA:
SHEILA BALLANTINE, JAN BASHFORD, JEAN COOKE.

PEOPLE OF ILLYRIA:
CHRISTOPHER BURGESS, SHEILA COOPER, PATIENCE GEE, BERNARD KAY, MICHAEL KEIR, LEE MONTAGUE, LEONARD MALEY, JOAN POULTER, REX ROBINSON, ELIZABETH ROGERS, PAMELA WICKINGTON, MARY WYLIE.

Scenery and Costumes by Roger Furse.
Music by Anthony Hopkins.

'If music be the food of love . . .'

[Photograph: John Vickers, London]

FESTE: Leo McKern, and ORSINO: Alec Clunes, with the Musicians serenade Olivia's house

'My father had a daughter loved a man'
ORSINO: Alec Clunes   VIOLA: Peggy Ashcroft

'I do assure you, 'tis against my will'
FABIAN: Paul Hansard   SIR ANDREW: Robert Eddison
VIOLA: Peggy Ashcroft   SIR TOBY: Roger Livesey

TWELFTH NIGHT

'This play is, in the grave parts, elegant and easy, and, in some of the lighter scenes, exquisitely humorous. Aguecheek is drawn with great propriety, but his character is, in great measure, that of natural fatuity, and is, therefore, not the proper prey of a satirist . . . The marriage of Olivia, and the succeeding perplexity, though well enough contrived to divert on the stage, wants credibility, and fails to produce the proper instruction required in the drama, as it exhibits no just picture of life.'

Thus does Dr. Johnson criticize the play we are to perform. We recognize that this is purely literary criticism and has no bearing on the effect of the play upon an audience. *Twelfth Night* has always been one of the most popular comedies in the language. The frequency of its performance by girls' schools and women's clubs has tended to make it a little too familiar in the eyes of the audience—too familiar for its magic to work easily on them.

But Johnson's criticism is interesting to the producer, if only because it takes as its criterion of judgement an entirely irrelevant standpoint, and so teaches us what not to do with the play. Johnson was steeped in the neo-classical tradition and judged this play by the standards of eighteenth-century comedy. Such standards demanded that the duty of comedy is to portray the excesses of human behaviour and to cure those excesses by laughing at them. Such comedy must have a moral and, however salacious its subject matter, a didactic purpose. What the critic is complaining about in this play is that there is no obvious moral to be drawn from *Twelfth Night*, and it cannot be regarded as a true picture of the way people behave. But it is, in fact, not a comedy of manners; it is a poetic comedy. Our job is not to caricature reality, but to create a world of fantasy. It is the poetic and, indeed, the fantastic quality of *Twelfth Night* that I want to emphasize in this production, for how else, except in terms of fantasy, are we to explain the delightful improbabilities of this story of a girl disguised as a boy and the incredible love story which ensues?

To emphasize the poetical quality of this play does not mean that I want the lines to be intoned in the manner of romantic acting, but it does mean that the sound of the play must be given its value, and that poetry must not be treated as an unnecessary decoration which comes between the actor and the characterization of his part. The modern tendency in Shakespearian performance to submit the characters to over-analytical treatment can be as harmful to the flow of the play, as the nineteenth-century tendency to intone the poetry and tear a passion to tatters with a fine display of oratory. Poetry must be spoken with meaning, but also with feeling; gestures and movement in a poetical play must be eloquent, and characterization must be kept within the bounds of poetic creation and not stray into the realm of naturalistic imitation. This play is a fantasy, it must hang in the air somewhere midway between earth and heaven.

Not all of *Twelfth Night* is written in poetry, and there may appear to be a large gulf between the lyrical characters of Orsino, Viola, Sebastian and Olivia, and the comic, earthy characters of Toby, Andrew, Malvolio and Maria. Too often in productions of *Twelfth Night* we see the clowns walking away with the play; in consequence, the lyrical people appear pale and even a little dull beside their boisterous, prosaic companions.

The Balance of the Play

Our main tasks must be: firstly, to balance the lyrical people with the comic people so that the latter do not outweigh the former; secondly, to weld these two elements together by creating a poetic world in which both can exist side by side.

Let us start with the problem of balancing the lyrical and the comic. The important thing to realize about the lyrical side of *Twelfth Night* is that it is comedy and not sentimentality. So often we see the characters of Orsino and Olivia played as sentimental, or straight, parts; as such they will appear poor acting material, particularly Orsino, and be easily submerged by the strong characters of Toby, Andrew, Malvolio and Maria. If this is the case, the play will be thrown off balance, the love story of Viola will lose our sympathy, and as for Olivia, she will become frankly a bore. Now, Orsino and Olivia are intended as satirical parts. Their satire is not, I admit, the full blooded comedy of the clowns which caught the fancy of the groundlings, but a more delicate comedy which delighted the gallants and their ladies in the galleries.

In the characters of Orsino and Olivia, Shakespeare is satirizing two affectations of his time. Orsino is the Elizabethan gallant who is in love with love, spending his time lolling on 'sweet beds of flowers' and contemplating an ideal mistress of his fancy. (The same type of self-indulgence is satirized in the young Romeo.) Olivia is the chaste Elizabethan beauty who is in love with grief, vowing she will never enjoy the society of man. Both these are, in Shakespeare's philosophy, unnatural states of mind and as such are laughable, and both were common enough affectations of court life in Shakespeare's time, as we find it reflected in Elizabethan and Jacobean love poetry. Neither Orsino nor Olivia are, in fact, sincere in their dedication, though both think they are. In contrast to their insincerity, Viola represents sincere love; the true, unaffected, natural, human passion which comes like a fresh breeze to blow away their conceits.

Now, once we have accepted this satire, the problem is how to make it tell without exaggerating the characters in such a way as to destroy their charm, for neither Orsino nor Olivia can be treated in the caricature fashion of Restoration drama. Shakespeare's satire is gentle satire, unlike the strongly marked satire of Dr. Johnson's ideal of comedy. The wistful smile graces his lips, not the full-throated laugh which we direct at the extravagant creatures of the comedy of Johnson's day. This satirical comedy is essentially human, and sympathy is extended to the affected persons. This gentle satire must, however, be marked, and both Orsino and Olivia must be accepted as part of the play's comedy. We will find, once we accept and play this satire, that the gulf between the lyrical people and the broader comics is not nearly so wide as would otherwise appear. Moreover, in playing this satire of insincerity, the sincerity of Viola stands out in its proper place as the embodiment of Shakespeare's own philosophy. This is a big step forward in balancing the seemingly diverse elements of the comedy.

To complete the balance of the play, however, there remains the problem of welding the comic and lyrical elements together by creating a poetic world in which both can exist side by side. The provision of a harmonizing background, in which the lyrical characters can exist beside the boisterous ones without hurt to either party, is of the utmost importance, otherwise we shall have two separate styles existing inside the comedy. If the two groups—the satirical and the broad comedy group—are not properly balanced, then, however much satire we infuse into the lyrical group we shall always find the comedy group predominant. The wittiest comedy by Oscar Wilde will fail to get its legitimate laughs if one of the characters spends his time slipping up on a banana skin, and no matter how discreetly we play Sir Toby Belch, we cannot escape the fact that he is the sort of person who has a prediliction for the type of humour which borders on farce. The background and atmosphere of the production must, therefore, provide the unifying factor and make it possible for broad comedy and satirical comedy to exist side by side. I will now turn to the way in which I intend, with the help of the designer, to treat the question of unification.

Setting and Costume

In *Twelfth Night*, as in all Shakespeare's fantastic comedies,

58

there is no accepted, normal state of society—the 'just picture of life' required by Dr. Johnson. In nearly every English comedy from Congreve to Coward the scene is laid in a contemporary setting, but in Shakespeare's fantastic comedies the author creates his own society, his own country and his own conduct of life. In these comedies we enter the kingdom of the high fantastical where the rules of behaviour and reason, in the eighteenth century or neo-classic sense, are left behind. It is significant that in only one of his comedies, *The Merry Wives of Windsor*, does Shakespeare choose an English background. Everywhere else we enter a fantastic country which is either an invention of his own—such as the Forest of Arden, Illyria, the Sea Coast of Bohemia—or a corner of the world sufficiently unknown to him and to his audience for a fantastic or unrealistic state of affairs to exist. In such a land of fantasy girls may be mistaken for boys, twins mixed up, lovers go to bed with each other without being aware of each other's identity, and many other incredible happenings take place. For such purposes his preference is for the old Italian romances which are laid in such places as Syracuse, Messina, Athens, and medieval France. He purposely avoids the contemporary society and the topical background, perhaps because it would have fettered his imagination and prescribed rules of behaviour too precise for his searching, poetic spirit. In this created world of fantastic comedy, anything can happen: Olivia can fall instantly in love with Viola and not be unduly perturbed when she finds that she has married Sebastian; Orsino can discover his love for Viola the moment he knows her to be a woman without any loss of the credibility so treasured by Dr. Johnson.

Twelfth Night is like nearly all Shakespeare's comedies, a comedy of love. But what distinguishes Illyria from the other fanciful countries of his comic genius is that it is a land of music. But Illyrian music is not only the food of love, it is also the food of every other kind of fancy; it sets free man's spirit to rove into the land of imagination, it opens the door of the kingdom of poetry, it induces melancholy and roisterous merriment and even tames the drunken clowns into a state of sentimentality. This land of Illyria, which is unfolded to us in Orsino's music with the dying fall and folded up again in Feste's song of the wind and the rain, rises like a magic island out of the sea, only to melt out of our grasp at the end like the land of fancy it is:

'But that's all one,
Our play is done,
And we'll strive to please you every day.'

To produce the true effect of this magic land of music on the stage we must free ourselves from the conventions which have stamped this play too strongly in the audiences' mind. We must try to find a new form in which to present the play. This form is all important, for to the modern playgoer it is not sufficient to return to the Elizabethan stage. We can no longer clothe the rush-strewn boards with our imagination, nor turn the Hall of the Middle Temple into the magic island of Illyria, as our Elizabethan ancestors were apparently able to do. Soaked as we are in the realism of the cinema and television, we require a greater impetus to set our imaginative faculties in motion and soar into Shakespeare's world of 'high fantastical', than did the playgoer of the Renaissance, to whom even such common objects as potatoes and pipes of tobacco were things of wonder, suggestive of incredible adventures. For us a spade is a spade, and the magic of Illyria can no longer exist in the Globe any more than it can exist in the box hedges of the overworked conventional setting of this play. The job of the modern designer of *Twelfth Night* is to find the right theatrical aids in order to allow his audience's imagination to reach across the centuries and find the magic world of Shakespeare's Illyria. The scenery of our production must be, therefore, neither conventional, nor realistic, nor purely Elizabethan, if it is to provide the right release for the imagination. It must be fresh, evocative and lyrical. This all important question is the designer's particular problem.

In searching for the form in which to present the play we have decided that certain principles must be born in mind: firstly, we must avoid unnecessary and cumbersome changes of scene; secondly, the poetic nature of the play can best be served by keeping as much of it in the open air as possible; thirdly, our scenery must be atmospheric without being realistic; lastly, we must give the play a sense both of intimacy and fantasy. This we have tried to do by placing Illyria on a small island off the Dalmatian coast. We realize it is an unconventional setting for the play, which is usually set among the trim box hedges of a typical Elizabethan garden—well enough, but no more than a recent theatrical convention when all is said. There are times when theatrical conventions should be broken; when the producer and designer should seek new visual aids for Shakespeare. *Twelfth Night* is, I believe, a case in point, for it is one of those plays which have become too familiar to the audience and it needs to be seen in a fresh light if its magic is to work again. But why choose the Dalmatian coast? First, because Dalmatia and the Aegean islands are probably Shakespeare's own geographical conception of where Illyria was, and, secondly, because when Viola and Sebastian are wrecked on a sea coast, we need some sort of fantasy island for them to arrive at. Moreover, though I place no great store by the source of the play, it is more than probable that it was derived from an old Italian play called Gl'Ingannati which stems from Venice and something of its Adriatic origin still lingers about it.

In pursuit of the principles outlined above we have arrived at the following three locations for the scenes:

1. *Act I, Sc. 1–4; Act II, Sc. 1–3; Act III, Sc. 3, and Act IV to end*

These scenes will be played in the piazza of a little seaport with streets leading to the sea, down which the shipwrecked travellers—Viola and Sebastian—will come. On either side of the piazza are the houses of Olivier and Orsino; neither of them very large or imposing, so as to maintain the feeling of a small, out of the way island, in which these two persons are the sole representatives of the aristocracy. In the middle of the piazza is a raised platform under which is the town prison.

2. *Act I, Sc. 5; Act II, Sc. 5; Act III, Sc. 2, and Act III, Sc. 4*

These scenes will be played in the garden of Olivia, a secluded spot screened by cypress trees, where this affected and wealthy lady can escape from the unwanted attention of her suitors.

3. *Act II, Sc.* 4

This most lovely of all the lyrical scenes will be played in the palace of Orsino, which we will treat in an airy Italianate fashion so as to preserve the open air character of the play.

We have given serious thought to the location of the drinking scene (Act II, Sc. 3). This is by tradition set in some kind of kitchen or cellar. Apart from our desire to avoid unnecessary scene changes, there is, as far as I can see, no indication in the text that this scene should take place in any definite locality. It can be played just as well immediately outside the door of Olivia's house, where the caterwauling of the knights would disturb the household no less than in the cellar. We have, therefore, decided to place this scene in the piazza at night, causing Toby and Andrew to enter as if returning from a carouse in the town, bearing a barrel of wine and a ladder with which Toby purposes to enter his niece's locked house through an upper window. Here they are joined by Feste, and the carouse becomes the merrier for a ladder and a barrel make an excellent see-saw. Maria and Malvolio issue from the house in a fruitless endeavour to prevent them from waking their mistress and causing Toby to be turned out for good.

Now the background we have described, revolving around the piazza of this small seaport, is reflected, though not in any pedantic sense, in the costumes. I would like you to imagine the inhabitants of Illyria as a gay, feckless, music-loving people, whose main occupation is the sea and all that pertains to it. If seafaring is the main occupation of the island, we can understand Orsino's anger with the pirate, Antonio. In such a community we will expect to find the common people dressed in simple, practical costumes, and the aristocrats in so small an island will be well-dressed but not over-ornate. Between the two households of Olivia and Orsino, there is not much to choose as far as wealth is concerned, and it is the natural expectation of the town that Olivia will in time ally herself with Orsino, there being no other suitable match for her on the island.

So much for what we might call the realism of our setting. I have, however, already indicated that the play cannot be treated realistically and must always move in the realms of the 'high fantastical'. The community we have outlined, therefore, only exists in the realms of the imagination. It is for this purpose that the designer has expressly avoided any definite period in the costume. It is for this purpose, too, that he has avoided any complete realism of setting, to which he has given an insubstantial quality in keeping with the fantasy of the story, for the play must remain timeless. To maintain this sense of timelessness and for the purpose of welding the lyrical and comic characters into a world where they can exist together, the designer has introduced into the costumes of Toby, Andrew, Feste, Malvolio and Fabian a marked note of the Commedia del Arte. In doing this we are not so wildly extravagant as it might seem, for the origins of this play were, as we have said, taken from an Italian source. This costume resemblance to the stock figures of Italian comedy is most predominant in the costumes of Feste and Fabian, about whom I shall have more to say later.

Having described the way in which we will try to give the play a unity and a fantastical atmosphere in keeping with its lyrical feeling, I will now pass to the question of characterization, which I will treat together with some indications of how I see the play appearing on the stage in this sort of setting.

Orsino

It is early morning when the curtain rises on the piazza of Illyria; the houses that surround it are silhouetted against the light of the rising sun. On our left is Olivia's house, on our right Orsino's palace. Asleep by the fountain in the centre is Feste, who, of course, has been out on the loose and has found himself locked out.

> 'Nay, either tell me where thou hast been, or I will not open my lips as wide as a bristle may enter, in way of thy excuse. My lady will hang thee for thy absence.'

In the distance a clock chimes and Feste wakes up, looking

apprehensively at Olivia's windows. He takes out his pipe and with a flourish summons the townspeople, who, as arranged, are to serenade Olivia on this fine summer's morning at the orders of Orsino; for Feste, as we find in Act II, Sc. 4, works for Orsino as well as Olivia. As the serenaders arrive and the music which is the 'food of love' is played beneath Olivia's windows, the door on the opposite side opens and Orsino, followed by his small retinue, enters.

The Duke of Illyria is the embodiment of the traditional lover with his sad, pale face, his Byronic collar, and his rich, flowing cloak. His eyes are fixed upon his mistress's closed shutters as he leans elegantly against the platform in the centre of the stage. He is the picture of an Elizabethan lover, but we must not imagine Orsino to be a spineless individual, nor purely a sentimental romantic. He is, in fact, a typical nobleman of Renaissance poetry and romance. He hunts, he likes music and poetry, he has a will of his own and a good deal of stubbornness. He is a man in search of the ideal. In his case this ideal takes the form of ideal love, and he has mistakenly embodied this ideal in the person of the dedicated virgin, Olivia. His love for her is as 'all embracing as the sea', and his passionate spirit is so absorbed with his imaginary ideal that he lives, acts and breathes love at every minute of the day. He requires only a good dose of liver salts, after which we shall find him a capital fellow and well worthy of Viola's love.

The music ended and the serenaders departed, he indulges in his favourite pastime of extolling his mistress:

'O! when mine eyes did see Olivia first,
Methought she purg'd the air of pestilence;
That instant was I turned into a hart,
And my desires, like fell and cruel hounds,
E'er since pursue me . . .'

The typical opening for one of those allegorical love sonnets, which were such favoured pursuits of the Elizabethan gentry. But he is interrupted by Valentine who, issuing from Olivia's house, comes to tell him that the chastity of his mistress has once again prevailed. Having received the daily refusal to his protestations of love, there is nothing to do but to spend the morning reclining on a nice bed of flowers, where the lover in love with love can indulge himself by reflecting on the cruelty of his ideal, and wholly imaginery, mistress.

Viola

And now as he passes across the stage a very different procession enters at the back, toiling wearily up the narrow streets from the sea. This is Viola with the sailors and the Sea Captain. 'What country, friends, is this?' Viola asks, as she stands in amazement watching the departure of the handsome, love-sick Duke and his dejected followers. The little group which has entered present a strong contrast to the previous occupants of the piazza. Wet-through, tired and dispirited, having spent the night struggling with the elements after the loss of their ship and of their dear ones, we see in them, and in particular in Viola, a sincere grief nobly borne, as opposed to the affected grief of Orsino. We notice how Viola is so overcome at the loss of her brother that she has no further wish to live. But how gradually her own courageous nature, awakened by the cheerful practicality of the Sea Captain, gains the upper hand, and she bravely determines to face a new life. It is this contrast between sincerity and insincerity, between true grief and affected grief, between true love and self-indulgence, which is the main theme of the play. These first two scenes are delicately balanced to emphasize this contrast. If we reverse them—which is sometimes argued to be theatrically effective—we destroy the delicacy with which the author has balanced his opening situation.

Now, so far we have pointed at Viola as being the acme of perfection in matters relating to the emotions in contrast to Orsino and Olivia. It is important, however, that, as well as recognizing her emotional sincerity, we also realize that she is a human being with a natural desire to gain the love of her lord. Viola is already on the way to being in love with Orsino when the play begins; for she has heard her father talk of him and she has conjured up a vision of this handsome bachelor Duke to which her girl's heart has responded. She is not, therefore, completely without ulterior motive in her decision to offer herself to his service. Does she hope to supplant Olivia in his affections? That would hardly be true at first, for she deliberately disguises herself as a boy. But Viola undoubtedly hopes that something will come of it all, and that the adventure, which is certainly a very bold move on her part, may prove rewarding. I do not mean that, when entrusted with her various love embassies on behalf of her master, she will lack diligence or prove deceitful, but once she sees that Olivia is adamant in her determination to reject her suitor, Viola does not hesitate to counsel Orsino to give up his useless passion, and there is more than a hint that he might look elsewhere for an outlet for his love in the mysterious tale:

> 'My father had a daughter lov'd a man,
>   As it might be, perhaps, were I a woman,
>   I should your lordship.'

Like the real woman she is, Viola likes to surround herself with a sense of mystery. Who is this strange youth who talks in riddles? She deliberately places a puzzle in Orsino's way for him to think out. It is the feminine side of Viola which makes us love her. She is not just an angel, incapable of the little deceits of human life. She is a woman in love. Her other human frailties only help to make her perfections more lovable. She is struck, for all her courage, with a very natural terror when asked to fight a duel. She has a delicious sense of irresponsibility which she assumes when things become too complicated and she finds that Olivia has fallen in love with her:

> 'O Time! thou must untangle this, not I;
>   It is too hard a knot for me to untie!'

Of all the characters that Shakespeare created, Viola is the most lovable, the most human.

Sir Toby Belch

And now that we have seen Viola off on her great adventure we can turn to the scene that follows. Sir Toby enters from Olivia's house, suffering from a bad hang-over, and thoroughly fed up with this endless state of mourning which pervades his niece's household. Seizing an opportunity to slip off unnoticed to the nearest hostelry, he is called back by Maria who has been watching him from Olivia's doorway. The two important points about Sir Toby Belch's character are: firstly, he is a gentleman who has run to seed; and secondly, he is quite determined he is going to enjoy life, no matter what other people want to do. The idea that he should confine himself within the modest limits of order is abhorrent to him:

'Confine? I'll confine myself no finer than I am:
These clothes are good enough to drink in, and so be these boots too.'

Toby is completely selfish, and hopelessly unsubtle in his selfishness. He plans to marry off his niece to the unsuitable Sir Andrew so that he can borrow money from the latter. He persuades this ninny of a suitor to fight Cesario so as to provide himself with a good entertainment. Anything that comes between him and his pleasures must be swept out of the way and the principal obstacle to his enjoyment of life is the sour face of the puritanical Malvolio. We might conclude from this that Toby is an unlikeable character, but in fact we like him because he is such a thorough rogue, and because he has such a constant, irrepressible sense of fun.

But with all his boisterousness, Toby must always remain a gentleman. In his most drunken moments we must see his ludicrous attempts to maintain his dignity. He is genuinely furious with the steward, Malvolio, for presuming to set himself up as a gentleman. The very fact that Toby was born a gentleman is his undoing. He has never had to work; he has been spoilt from his youth, and he has always managed to bluster his way through life. The new regime of cloistered virginity, which has been adopted by his niece since the death of her brother and the consequent dominance of Malvolio, has caused him to break out more wildly than ever as a protest against petticoat government in particular, and puritanism in general. For this we cannot wholly blame him; and for the understanding of Toby's behaviour we see one more reason why Olivia's character must be gently satirized. It is her affectations as much as Toby's own weakness which causes his excessive behaviour. You cannot confine Sir Toby Belch in a cloister of affected grief, where the vows and company of men have been abjured. He has learned to spend his money recklessly, to drink, to quarrel, and to dance. His trouble is that he is now penniless and dependent on his niece for his clothes and food. No wonder he cultivates Aguecheek for the sake of a little financial independence.

Maria

For Maria, who tries to keep Toby on the rails, we may say that, apart from being Olivia's gentlewoman, she is the brains behind Toby. We imagine her as a high-spirited and neat person. She has come to be a little mother to Toby, trying to conceal his worst extravagances and save him from Olivia's tongue. But she is no doormat to be walked on by him, which would undoubtedly be her fate were she not possessed of a ready wit, a considerable courage, and a great sense of mischief. All these features make her into an indispensable prop for the rather helpless, old rascal for whom she cannot help but feel affection.

Although Maria has plenty of sound sense she is by no means beyond encouraging Toby to mischief, especially where Malvolio is concerned. We can easily imagine that the position of overbearing authority, which this intolerable steward has assumed in the household since the death of Olivia's brother, has not only made Toby far more truculent than usual, but has also made the servants, Maria, Feste and Fabian, ripe for revolt. They are all ready for mischief and Maria is determined to use it to bring about Malvolio's downfall. For this purpose she encourages Toby and supplies him with a device to overthrow this household tyrant. The fact that Toby marries her out of gratitude was probably a nice piece of calculation on Maria's part. But their marriage is as happy an augury for Toby's future as we can imagine, for it is highly unlikely that anyone else would have accepted the penniless, old reprobate, and, if anyone could keep Toby within the confines of some kind of order, Maria is the person to do it. Their marriage will undoubtedly be considered a misalliance in aristocratic circles. I hardly imagine Maria will be received at Orsino's court, but I feel quite sure that they never wanted for company round their hearth, nor did the company ever want for a 'stoup of wine', or a witty word from their hostess.

Sir Andrew Aguecheek

And 'here comes Sir Andrew Aguecheek' on his way to pursue his preposterous courtship of Olivia. A more unlikely suitor for that temperamental Prima Donna's hand we cannot imagine. Perhaps Sir Andrew lives on the other side of the island of Illyria, but more likely he lives in the more cultured city of Venice, where he has learned to play the viol-de-gamboys and to speak 'three or four languages word for word without book'. At all events, he has plenty of money and is, as Maria says, 'a very fool and a prodigal'.

He has come to the little town of Illyria to woo the rich heiress, obviously at the instigation of Sir Toby, who hopes to reap a rich harvest from the match; for Sir Andrew is completely under the thumb of his boisterous companion. Toby is a fatal attraction to the timorous, weak-brained Andrew. In Toby's presence Sir Andrew feels himself a bit of a blood. Such is his need for an inflation of his ego that he will follow this bully-boy round like a spaniel, no matter how many kicks he receives; rejoicing in any little spark of encouragement that may fall from the old rogue's lips. He is one of those totally vacant-brained gentlemen who can be counted on to put his foot in it on every occasion; yet there is no malice in him, but rather a pathetic desire to please everyone and above all a wish to be thought well of, which invariably results in his making a fool of himself. He is aware that he is a bit of a failure, which occasionally makes him melancholy, and without the constant encouragement of Toby's companionship, he would give up at once.

This companionship between the old rogue and his fatuous hanger-on is not purely a matter of a desire for money on the one side and for inflation of ego on the other. Toby and

Andrew have a strange affection for each other, and always back each other up when either is criticized. We should feel that, despite the difference of age and temperament, they are firm friends. But Andrew has just enough spark in him to revolt occasionally against Toby's dominance. Unfortunately it never comes to anything, for his courage is very slight, and a comforting word from his idol makes him a 'dear mannikin' once more. The quality which really endears Andrew to us is that he knows what a pitiful fellow he is. His desire to take part in everything, his valiant attempts to impress Toby with his courage, his happiness when Toby praises his prowess in dancing, his pathetic confession that he was 'loved once, too', all make of this poor num-skull a thoroughly lovable, if always ludicrous, creature.

So Toby and Andrew dance away from the piazza to set about some revels and for a few hours Andrew will bask in the sunshine of Toby's companionship. They are followed by Viola and Orsino's lords and there is more than a hint of jealousy in Valentine's lines to Viola:

> 'If the Duke continue these favours towards you, Cesario, you are like to be much advanced.'

For she has won Orsino's confidence, and now it is Viola and not Valentine who will be entrusted with the embassies of love. Viola goes off on her first embassy to Olivia accompanied by 'some four or five', and as they go the scene is changed from the piazza into Olivia's garden. When the music ends and the change is completed, we see Feste trying to elude Maria as she chases him in and out of the Illyrian boys and girls who have aided the change of scene. By the device of changing the scene in front of the audience, using the inhabitants of the island to move the pieces around, we will hope to maintain the flow of the play, and at the same time by the use of music maintain its fantastic character.

Feste

I will begin by describing what is realistic about the character of Feste before I pass to what I might describe as the fantasy of his part. Feste is a sort of half-way person, belonging partly to the plot of the play, and partly to the strange musical atmosphere in which it is wrapped. The realistic Feste is the Feste of Olivia's household. He is a little, middle-aged creature who lives by his clowning, by his songs, by his ability to amuse his patroness. The existence of a licensed fool was probably a most precarious form of earning a living, for to be successful a fool has always to be able to produce the required distraction, no matter what his private feelings might be. Professional fooling required a daring and an impudence of approach which, if taken amiss by the uncertain temper of a patron, resulted in a beating at the best, or a hanging at the worst. More often failure to strike the right note entailed dismissal and we may be sure that a fool had little ability to earn his living at anything else.

Feste lives under this constant threat of dismissal; for Olivia with her affected grief is a very uncertain customer to serve. Moreover, it is clear that he is no longer quite equal to his job; perhaps he is growing old and a little stale.

> 'Now you see, sir, how your fooling grows old,
> and people dislike it'

says Olivia to him, and Feste, unable to make any reply to this, quickly changes the subject. Now, if Feste is in danger of losing his job because his fooling is beginning to pall, he has two additional pitfalls to contend with: one is Malvolio, and the other his own irrepressible nature. Between him and Olivia's steward there is a constant feud; for not only is Malvolio bitterly jealous of any intimacy between his mistress and another servant, but as a Puritan and a man completely devoid of humour he has an inborn distaste for, as well as a strong distrust of, Feste's jests. Feste is quite aware of Malvolio's hostility and he knows, too, that the steward will do his utmost to get him thrown out of service. Feste's ultimate cruel mockery of the distracted Malvolio is only understood if we realize how serious a threat the steward is to Feste's livelihood. In the first scene when we see them together Malvolio administers a stinging insult to the ageing jester:

'I saw him put down the other day with an ordinary fool,
that has no more brain than a stone.'

Feste is at once touched to the quick; his professional pride has
been badly wounded—put down by an ordinary fool! Is he
losing his grip on his job? He is haunted by this cruel gibe and,
when it is Malvolio's turn to lose favour, back comes these
words out of Feste's mouth:

'But do you remember? "Madam, why laugh you at such
a barren rascal?"'

and so 'the whirligig of time brings in his revenges'.

The other pitfall that Feste has to contend against is his own
irrepressible high spirits. Like Toby, Feste cannot confine
himself within the modest limits of order. He is always out on
the loose, not necessarily drinking, like Toby, but enjoying
himself, flitting from place to place, sometimes at Orsino's
house, sometimes in the company of Toby and Andrew. We
shall see him in this production dancing with the music-loving
crowd, mocking Orsino's sentimentality and getting into every
sort of mischief, when he should be at home pandering to
Olivia's whims. At the end he has gone too far—Olivia
promises to right Malvolio's wrongs:

'But when we know the grounds and authors of it, thou
shalt be both the plaintiff and the judge of thine own
cause.'

This threat of an investigation into Malvolio's imprisonment
cannot fail to produce fatal evidence against Feste, who is not
only Malvolio's main enemy, but is also the most vulnerable
of his mockers; for he cannot be allowed the liberty of Sir Toby
and Sir Andrew, and Maria is safely married. Thus it is that
when the happy couples go off to celebrate their 'solemn
combination' Feste is left behind, and his last song has an omi-
nous significance in its refrain of 'the wind and the rain'.

About the fantasy of Feste's part I shall have something to
say later, but I will now turn to Olivia as she enters her garden
accompanied by her dutifully sad ladies.

Olivia

I have already spoken of Olivia's insincerity, but I do not wish to give the impression that she is incapable of sincere love. We must imagine that this chaste lady is confronted with a considerable problem owing to Orsino's insistent wooing of her. She comes of a proud, rich family and we maintain that on this island there is no other suitable husband at hand, for she cannot take Sir Andrew's suit seriously. Unfortunately she does not love Orsino, and it is partly in self-defence that she affects a life of cloistered seclusion, hiding behind vows of everlasting mourning for her dead brother. She is, of course, quite aware that this form of prevarication makes her the more attractive to Orsino; aware, too, of her personal charms, as she clearly shows when she makes an inventory of her beauty to Viola:

'Item, two lips indifferent red.'

Olivia has no intention of remaining a nun all her life, but it is a pleasant conceit for the moment, and, whilst holding Orsino at bay, she can, from behind her veil, be on the look-out for a nice personable young man. The joke of this situation is, of course, that she falls head over heels in love with Cesario, who is unable to respond. Thus she is placed in the most embarrassing position of having to endure the same scornful rejection of her own love as she has dealt out to Orsino.

This gentle comedy of the scornful beauty who rejects and is rejected will only become apparent if from the first the actress has struck the right note of affectation. If, on the contrary, the audience have been led to accept Olivia as a charming, straight juvenile, the comedy will be lost, the part appear insipid, and the pursuit of Viola-Cesario indecent and undecorous. Olivia is, of course, dressed in black and heavily veiled, her manner is one of assumed grief, which she manages to make very attractive. Behind the veil there is more than a hint of a self-willed, temperamental flirt and we should find no small degree of comedy in the haste with which she whips Sebastian off to church, before he has time to look round. The secret of the acting of Olivia is to balance affectation with

73

attraction, and to underline the gentle, but unmistakable comedy of this capricious young woman, who woos so assiduously a girl under the impression that she has found a gallant, young gentleman.

Malvolio

In her steward, Malvolio, who accompanies her into the garden, we recognize the mixture of the Puritan and the proud servant who aspires to greatness. Since the death of Olivia's brother, Malvolio has clearly seen a golden opportunity for advancing both his authority and his social position. Olivia's affected grief has placed some good cards in his hands; for, as her principal male confidant, he is able to exert his authority over her household without interference, and who knows how far his advancement may carry him:

> 'There is example for't; the lady of the Strachy
> married the yeoman of the wardrobe.'

Malvolio is in love with his mistress, or at all events he has imagined himself to be so. He is a very ambitious person and, in his determination to keep Olivia to himself, he encourages her to reject all suitors with the utmost diligence. But although he concurs with Olivia's affectation of chaste seclusion, he does not entirely approve of his mistress's taste. He thoroughly disapproves of her championship of Feste, her tolerance of Toby and her dangerous interest in Cesario. We can well imagine his dislike at being asked to carry a ring from his mistress to this young stripling, Cesario, after his visit to Olivia. We can understand with what excitement he reads the letter that Maria drops in his path, and we can see how completely his ambition and pride are overthrown when he discovers the hoax that has been played on him.

Malvolio is, however, not a figure of tragedy, nor yet a fearsome villain. He is an intolerably pompous person, and as such he is exceedingly funny. He is puffed up with pride, credulous to a degree, full of affectations and fine airs and utterly lacking in any sense of humour, the absence of which makes him an easy butt for the 'lesser people'. He is, in fact, the sort of person who always gets his leg pulled, because he never sees a joke, and deserves to get his leg pulled, because he dislikes any form of fun in others. His gait, his dress, his speech, his pride, his 'austere regard' and his officiousness earn him the mockery that is meted out to him, and although his punishment is a little cruel by our standards, we must remember that these Elizabethan Illyrians were more full-blooded than we are.

We picture him as a middle-aged governess of a creature who folds his clothes meticulously when he goes to bed, and probably pins up his hair. No doubt he suffers severely from corns and objects very strongly to being told to hurry:

'Run after that same peevish messenger.'

We can imagine with what a look of surprised hauteur Malvolio receives this instruction from his mistress to unbend his dignity and take to his heels! He passes from the play like an enraged hen with his feathers not a little ruffled, but with his self-conceit untouched.

Sebastian and Antonio

I will now turn from the group in the garden to two other figures who later enter the piazza: Sebastian and Antonio. About the former there is not a great deal to say, except that he is a thoroughly likeable young man who shares the same sort of directness that we find in his twin sister, Viola. Sebastian has an openness about him, an innate honesty, and a freshness which immediately endears him to his older companion. Like Viola he is deeply affected by the loss of his twin, but he has the same courageous determination to start life again and to seek his fortune cheerfully. He is the sort of person who responds very quickly to his emotions. He warms at once to Antonio's kindness; he falls head over heels in love with Olivia, and he does not hesitate to draw his sword on Andrew and Toby. The very quickness of his emotional response make him hot tempered as well as warm-hearted. Above all, the actor who plays Sebastian must approach the part lyrically. The joyous soliloquy 'This is the air, that is the glorious sun . . .' and the infinitely tender recognition of Viola demand a lyrical approach to the acting of this part which is of great importance to our acceptance of what might otherwise appear improbable.

There must be something about these twins that makes them specially attractive to the tougher type of male, for just as Viola wins the devotion of the Sea Captain, so Sebastian captures the affection of the pirate, Antonio. The secret of this attraction lies, I think, in the directness and warmth of their youthful affections. There is nothing complicated or affected in them to make the rough sea-dogs feel out of their depth. They bring out the fathering instinct, which is often a very endearing characteristic of the hardened seaman.

Antonio is a thorough seaman; honest and straightforward in his personal dealings, generous with his purse, despising meanness and ingratitude, brave in combat, incapable of cloaking his feelings when angered, and a devil when it comes to a scrap. He has, like Drake and Grenfell, been a notable pirate attacking with his 'bawbling vessel' the 'most noble bottom' of Orsino's fleet. Antonio denies this charge of piracy. To his way of thinking he won his prizes in fair combat with the odds against him, but he realizes that he may be justly regarded as Orsino's enemy, for, whereas his compatriots handed back their pirated gains in order to conclude an advantageous trade pact with the government of Illyria, Antonio refused to do so. He is, therefore, a marked man in Illyria; well knowing the danger he runs in accompanying Sebastian through the streets. It is clear that he must not walk, as Sebastian says, 'too open'; there must always be a cautiousness in his movements, as if he were constantly on the look-out for trouble. It is only when he sees what he thinks to be his young charge in bodily danger that he throws caution to the wind and rushes headlong into action and so into the arms of Orsino's officers. From then on he behaves as we would expect him to, in a fearless and courageous manner. We know he would walk with his head up to the gallows, were he not ultimately rescued by Sebastian.

Fabian, the Clown?

So far we have covered all the main characters of this play

with the exception of Fabian. Here lies a problem. Who is this unexpected and unexplained character?

We had been led to believe from the plot concocted by Maria and Toby that the clown would make a third in the trapping of Malvolio. It is, therefore, not a little surprising that Shakespeare discards his clear intention that Feste should accompany Toby and Andrew in the letter scene, and deliberately replaces him with a character called Fabian, whose sole explanation of himself is that Malvolio 'brought him out of favour' with his mistress, Olivia, about a bear-baiting. Many explanations have been offered for the inclusion of this apparently unnecessary part, which seems to have been intended at one stage of the writing to be contained in the part of Feste, the clown. Perhaps the reason is that the actor who played Feste got a little beyond himself at rehearsals, and, as a result, the original Malvolio complained about the number of pranks that were being played behind his back whilst he was reading the letter, and insisted that Feste's part be given to another. Let the actor of Feste take note! Whatever the truth may be, we are now forced to accept the inclusion of Fabian, since from the letter scene onwards he takes an integral part in the action. It remains for us to find an explanation for him.

Licence, if it be in keeping with the spirit of the play, is perhaps allowed in the interpretation of Fabian. I propose to play him as a second clown—a rival to the ageing Feste. Like Feste he is a member of Olivia's household, but he is younger and less extravagant in his behaviour. If he be a clown, then with reasonable luck he may hope to succeed his rival, for his high spirits are more strictly under control. When Feste is asked to read Malvolio's letter to Olivia in the last scene of the play, he earns her rebuke for his ridiculous way of doing so, and she tells Fabian to read it instead. We can imagine how Feste's professional pride would bridle at this rebuke, which coupled with the facts that it is to another clown the letter is given and that this rival has already supplanted him in Toby's affection, will do much to emphasize Feste's final bitter clash with Malvolio, as being the only person on whom he can vent his hurt feelings.

This interpretation will help, too, in making Feste's last

song of the wind and the rain more poignant, for not only has he lost his place, but his successor has probably already been found.

Feste, the Pivot of the Play

I would like, at this point, to return to Feste as I said I would, and point out that although this song of the wind and the rain has a special poignancy when related to Feste's position, I do not want it sung sentimentally. Feste is not a sentimentalist. If fortune has dealt cruelly with him, he does not mope and die like Jack Point in *The Yeomen of the Guard*. He should attack it with a pace and bravado which make it all the more poignant, for we know that his situation belies his words. We must know, too, that this song is half-way between the realistic Feste, the licensed fool of Olivia, and the fantastic Feste, the commentator upon the play.

Shakespeare wrote *Twelfth Night* with music sounding round him, and Feste with his songs is the author's principal instrument for introducing music into the play. To this extent, therefore, he has a role outside the normal characterization of his part. Moreover, the clown in the Elizabethan tradition was half-way between a straight actor and a licensed comedian, a relic of the devils of the mystery plays on the one hand and a borrowing from the Italian comedies on the other. I do not wish to pursue this theme beyond explaining why I intend to use Feste in his guise of Arlechino to punctuate the action. In this sort of dual role—realistic and fantastic—he is supported by the crowd of Illyrian girls and boys who represent both the inhabitants of Illyria on the realistic side and convey, as creatures of fantasy, the atmosphere of music and dance which will characterize the treatment of this production.

To these people falls the task of conveying Viola on her journeys to and from Olivia's garden and at the same time changing the scenery as they pass along their route. At the same time, like Feste, they have a realistic role to play, and as Orsino's subjects they take part in the action, more especially in the latter part of the play, where the excitement of the final discoveries will be enhanced by their presence. Now the use of a crowd of this nature in *Twelfth Night* will need careful and tactful handling if it is not to degenerate into the chorus of a musical comedy. Our task will be to use the music and dances to enhance the fantasy without allowing them to become extraneous to the flow and action of the play. The success of their presence will depend on our ability to keep the whole play within the realms of the 'high fantastical' without losing touch with the true characterization of these delightful creatures.

This balance of fantasy and reality is important. I have already stressed that *Twelfth Night* is a lyrical comedy, not a comedy of manners. It lives in the half-way house between reality and unreality, and although I have tried to describe the characters to you from the realistic point of view, I want you to play them with a lyrical approach so as to lift them off the ground and allow the whole play to move in the sphere of poetry.

For *Twelfth Night* is a magic play, written by the poet at the height of his powers before the intense bitterness of his great tragic period swept over him. It is withal a completely mature play. We do not have to contend with the obscure conceits and puns of *Love's Labour's Lost*, nor the paste-board characterization of *The Shrew*. The plot is carefully balanced, the characters warm and alive, the verse and prose have the rounded character of an author who is writing in full control of his pen. The playing of it is a challenge to our imagination and to our powers of delicate and subtle distinction of comedy. It demands the full intelligence and acting experience of a company—no more than that, of a team of first class players.

POSTSCRIPT

The occasion for which this production was designed was the re-opening of the Old Vic in November 1950. Ten years before that date the theatre had been bombed and the company rendered homeless. Now after many wanderings, it had come home. Emotion and excitement ran high on the opening night, as we waited back-stage for the all-clear signal from the front. Outside a large crowd of the inhabitants of the Lower Marsh and the Cut had gathered to witness the unfamiliar invasion of mink stoles, evening dress and expensive cars.

On stage we had our own secret, for Edith Evans had flown from New York to speak a prologue specially written for the occasion by Christopher Hassall.

It might be argued that such an occasion demanded a more conventional performance of *Twelfth Night* than we were to give, but I remain unrepentant. When preparing the production I found it impossible to conceive this play in the hackneyed setting of nineteenth-century convention. This was a new chapter in the life of the Old Vic, it required a fresh approach. Moreover the new stage of the Vic, which had abolished the picture-frame and added a large projecting platform, required a new treatment. On this stage the main acting area is no longer behind the curtain line, but in front of it. The actors can no longer play within the boundaries of the scenery and all pretences to reality are destroyed. It is a compromise between the illusionist stage and the formalized Elizabethan, it is, in fact, more akin to the Restoration stage than to either. But the picture scenery of the Restoration theatre is totally out of sympathy with our own age and with Shakespeare's. The problem, therefore, consists of finding a convention which is neither illusionist, nor purely formal. The designer solved this problem from the point of view of *Twelfth Night* by providing scenery, which had the insubstantial and fantastic quality with which I was seeking to endow the production. The houses that backed the piazza were constructed on light frames suspended on wires, so that they could sink down in sight of the audience when the scene changed to Olivia's garden. To preserve the fantasy of the play the scene changes were effected by the actors.

The colour scheme of greys, pinks and pale blues gave a feeling of lightness. Perhaps we made too much play with our crowd of music-loving inhabitants, which provided some critics with the opportunity of indulging in that type of journalist's wit which so often takes the place of reasoned criticism. Nevertheless, the device was in keeping with the festive character which is an important aspect of the play. Why else is it called *Twelfth Night*, if it be not because it was written for that festival? It is a festive play—a fantasy of music, love and incredibility. It is our mistaken form of reverence for Shakespeare, together with the lingering traditions of Johnson's age of didactic moralizing, that have perverted our vision of this comedy and made our critics hold up their hands in horror at the libertines who fantasticate the Bard.

THE MERRY WIVES OF WINDSOR

THE MERRY WIVES OF WINDSOR
Old Vic Theatre Company

31st May 1951

SIR JOHN FALSTAFF	ROGER LIVESEY
FORD	ALEC CLUNES
PAGE	DOUGLAS CAMPBELL
SHALLOW	WILLIAM DEVLIN
SLENDER	ROBERT EDDISON
SIR HUGH EVANS	MARK DIGNAM
DOCTOR CAIUS	PAUL ROGERS
FENTON	PAUL HANSARD
HOST OF THE GARTER INN	RUPERT DAVIES
BARDOLPH ⎫	⎧ JOHN BLATCHLEY
PISTOL ⎬ *Followers of Falstaff*	⎨ DOUGLAS WILMER
NYM ⎭	⎩ LEO MCKERN
ROBIN, *Page of Falstaff*	BRIAN SMITH
SIMPLE, *Servant of Slender*	RICHARD PASCO
RUGBY, *Servant of Dr. Caius*	PETER DUGUID
JOHN ⎫ *Servants of Mrs. Ford*	⎧ JAMES GROUT
ROBERT ⎭	⎩ JOHN WALKER
MISTRESS FORD	URSULA JEANS
MISTRESS PAGE	PEGGY ASHCROFT
ANNE PAGE	DOROTHY TUTIN
MISTRESS QUICKLY	NUNA DAVEY

TOWNSPEOPLE AND SERVANTS:
SHEILA BALLANTINE, JAN BASHFORD, STANLEY BLACK-MAN, CHRISTOPHER BURGESS, MARGARET CHISHOLM, SHEILA COOPER, DAVID COOTE, LAWRENCE DAVIDSON, PATIENCE GEE, TREVOR HILL, BERNARD KAY, MICHAEL KEIR, LEONARD MALEY, BRIAN MATTHEW, LEE MONTAGUE, JOAN POULTER, REX ROBINSON, ELIZABETH ROGERS, PAMELA WICKINGTON, MARY WYLIE.

Costumes and Scenery by Alan Barlow.
Music composed by Clifton Parker.

The Merry Wives

MISTRESS PAGE: Peggy Ashcroft   MISTRESS FORD: Ursula Jeans

[Photograph: John Vickers, London

MISTRESS PAGE: Peggy Ashcroft   FALSTAFF: Roger Livesey
ROBIN: Brian Smith   MISTRESS FORD: Ursula Jeans

[Photograph: John Vickers, London

'I shall be with her between ten and eleven'
FALSTAFF: Roger Livesey   FORD, alias Brook: Alec Clunes

THE MERRY
WIVES OF WINDSOR

IN the early eighteenth century, when eye-witness accounts of Shakespeare and his fellow actors were still within living memory, it was generally held that this play was written at the direct command of Queen Elizabeth, who had been so delighted with the character of Sir John Falstaff that she desired to see that knight in love. Some commentators maintain that the play was written in a fortnight; '. . . a prodigious thing, when all is so well contrived, and carried on without the least confusion'.

Whether these facts are true or not matters little to the acting of it, but unlike most of the Shakespeare legends, this one seems to me reasonably probable, and may explain why Mistress Quickly treats us to that unexpected and somewhat naïve eulogy of the Order of the Garter in the last scene:

'And nightly, meadow fairies, look you sing,
Like to the Garter's compass, in a ring;
Th' expressure that it bears, green let it be,
More fertile fresh than all the field to see;
And *Honi soit qui mal y pense* write
In emerald tufts, flowers purple, blue and white;
Like sapphire, pearl, and rich embroidery,
Buckled below fair knighthood's bending knee:'

This salute to the royal order of chivalry, together with the fact that the plot is laid in Windsor and not in some imaginery country, like the other Shakespeare comedies, may indeed have been a compliment to the Queen who ordered it, and in front of whom it was perhaps first performed.

The theory that it was hastily written (though possibly a fortnight is an exaggeration) seems also to have some substance, and would explain why it is written almost entirely in prose, and why, when it breaks into verse, the poetry is particularly weak. Pressure of time would also explain some gross inconsistencies in the text and the erratic progress of the action, which lacks the cumulative flow of the greater comedies. Some critics have seized on the made-to-order legend to excuse their disappointment at what they consider the deflation of Falstaff, and of this matter I would like to speak for a moment.

Dr. Johnson says, 'No task is harder than that of writing to the ideas of another. Shakespeare knew what the queen, if the story be true, seems not to have known, that by any real passion of tenderness, the selfish craft, the careless jollity, and the lazy luxury of Falstaff must have suffered so much abatement, that little of his former cast would have remained. Falstaff could not love, but by ceasing to be Falstaff. He could only counterfeit love, and his professions could be prompted, not by the hope of pleasure, but of money . . .'; and Hartley Coleridge in the nineteenth century says: 'That Queen Bess should have desired to see Falstaff making love proves her to have been, as she was, a gross-minded old baggage . . . Falstaff of *The Merry Wives* is not the Falstaff of *Henry IV*. It is a big-bellied impostor.'

Now such critics must be regarded seriously, if they represent public opinion. It should be noted, however, that they do not condemn the character of a fat, old knight in love; their criticism is directed at the lack of consistency between the fat knight of *The Merry Wives* and the fat knight of the histories. They bemoan the deflation of Falstaff of *Henry IV*, rather than condemn the character who appears in this play. The question is should we endeavour to confute such opinions by trying to present a Sir John who is a true sequel to the Sir John of *Henry IV*, or should we forget all about that sly, old rogue and present *The Merry Wives of Windsor* as if *Henry IV* had never been written.

To try to reconcile the two Falstaffs would, in my opinion, be impossible, since the author has not endowed the character of Falstaff in *The Merry Wives* with the same qualities, or if you prefer it defects, as the character in the histories. There is no reason why the actor of Falstaff in this play should regret this lack of consistency with the earlier character; it is a purely literary affair and has nothing to do with acting. The critics who deplore the metamorphosis of their favourite character concentrate their criticism on the fact that Falstaff of *Henry IV* would never have allowed himself to become a dupe of anyone, let alone of a couple of mischievous ladies, but they do not deny that the dupe is a perfectly acceptable character in his own right, whose antics would have pleased them well enough if only he hadn't been called Falstaff. In short, this criticism of *The Merry Wives* is literary, not dramatic. Like the critics of *The Merchant of Venice*, the critics of *The Merry Wives* are unable to explain why so weak a literary effort should be so popular a play. We should, therefore, present *The Merry Wives of Windsor* as a play in its own right, and, despite its obvious weakness, recognize it as a piece which has always been beloved by the groundlings. We should not try to link it with the history cycle. That is the first point I want to make about this production.

The second point is that *The Merry Wives* is a contemporary domestic comedy; the only comedy of its kind that Shakespeare wrote. The scene is laid in Windsor, not on the sea coast of Bohemia, nor in a wood near Athens. Moreover, it is the Windsor of Shakespeare's own day; the Windsor of Queen Elizabeth, not the Windsor of Henry Bolingbroke and mad Prince Hal. There are those who would place these events in the life of Falstaff between *Henry IV Part II* and *Henry V*, namely after the disgrace of Falstaff and before his death and the dispersal of his retainers. There is, however, nothing in the text of the play to suggest that Shakespeare had any chronology of Falstaff's life in mind. Except for a remark of Page's, which refers to Fenton as having kept company with the wild

Prince and Poines, there is no link with the previous history plays, except the names of the characters themselves. It is a separate action, divorced from history.

The background of this play is not the insurrections and wars which characterized the reigns of *Henry IV* and *V*, but the good living, the country sports, the sense of security, which distinguished the reign of Queen Elizabeth. We are living among a people who are free from fear, in a country at peace, where trade flourishes and food abounds; not in an atmosphere of political unrest, where kings' consciences are burdened with the murder of their predecessors and where bishops and barons are intriguing for power. *The Merry Wives of Windsor* represents the merry life of England; the England we love best to remember; the England of country sports, blazing fires, inns dispensing good cheer, of rich parkland and of old wives' tales:

'There is an old tale goes that Herne the hunter,
Sometimes a keeper here in Windsor forest,
Doth all the winter-time at still midnight
Walk round about an oak, with great ragg'd horns:'

So the second point I want to make about the production is that this is an Elizabethan play, despite its references to the mad Prince and Poines, and we will play it in an Elizabethan costume and setting. This will, I hope, help to separate the Falstaff of *The Merry Wives* from his namesake in *Henry IV* and, perhaps, do something to appease his critics.

My third point is that it is a play about middle-class society. We are not presenting kings and queens and cardinals, nor does the stage resound to the proud call of the trumpet. The principal protaganists are misters and mistresses, with the exception of Sir John Falstaff and Sir Hugh Evans, neither of whom occupy an important position in affairs of state, or, indeed, in the social scale. Now the importance of this is considerable. We are acting a comedy by Shakespeare in which we are not asked to portray the court of a King of Bohemia or Navarre, nor a Duke of Illyria or Athens. The play is set fairly and squarely in a realistic social order, a society that was well known to Shakespeare and his fellow actors, a society that may claim to be the backbone of our national life from 1550 to 1950.

The point, therefore, that arises is that we must interpret this social life realistically and domestically, taking note of, and giving point to, the social conditions contained in it. Let us, therefore, for a moment, examine this social order as it is portrayed in this, the only wholly contemporary Elizabethan play from Shakespeare's pen.

Social Background

The end of the sixteenth century was a period of considerable prosperity and stability in English life. The power of the barons had been curbed, the Church had been subordinated to the throne, and the country as a whole had turned for the first time for many hundreds of years to the cultivation of its natural wealth and to the ways of peace. The lords, tamed and deprived of their private armies, were transformed into courtiers surrounding and administering to the sovereign, who, instead of being an indifferently rich feudal prince, dependent on the support of Church and barons, had become a sort of Queen Bee at the apex of national life. The old feudal barons were being transformed into a race of drones, and were becoming remote from the life of the country. Instead of administering their estates personally they had gone to court, where they became the gorgeous butterflies, caparisoned in the bejewelled fashion of Nicholas Hillyard's miniatures.

The task of maintaining stability and social order had passed out of their hands and out of the hands of the church, and was rapidly falling into the hands of the commons, that is into the hands of the merchants and sheep farmers who brought prosperity to the towns and fields. This new middle-class was to frame the policy of the country for the next three hundred years. Class distinctions were, however, nothing like as marked under the wise rule of Elizabeth as they were to become in later years. The younger sons of the aristocracy were turned adrift by their families to seek employment in trade or the liberal professions, and to make their own way in the world.

The merchant class was proud of its industry and of its newly-won prosperity, being, in the main, an intensely respectable, church-going society which frowned upon the frivolities and extravagances of the courtiers.

In *The Merry Wives* we see typical examples of both these points—the lack of acute class distinctions on the one hand, and the growing pride and respectability of the middle-class on the other. The families of Master Page and Master Ford are the embodiment of the new hard core of national life, whilst Falstaff is an exaggerated example of the decayed aristocratic tradition. Falstaff, like many other knights who believed in the old order, had failed to transform himself into a peaceful squire or a polished courtier, and had squandered his diminished patrimony on riotous living. This adventurous way of life has turned him into a thorough rogue, surrounded by a crew of disbanded soldiers who earn their living by low cunning, powerfully aided by sleight of hand. His amorous desires are strongly influenced by his interest in the wealth that lies sealed up in the comfortable houses of these middle-class ladies:

'Now the report goes she has all the rule of her husband's purse: he hath a legion of angels.'

When the opportunities of making money out of the old disturbed state of the realm are denied him, Falstaff turns to the new treasure house of the merchants' money bags.

Fenton is another type of aristocrat, one of the resplendent throng which surrounded the Queen at Whitehall and Windsor. He, too, is interested in the money bags of the merchant classes, for the life of a courtier was excessively expensive:

'Albeit I will confess thy father's wealth
Was the first motive that I woo'd thee, Anne.'

Unlike Falstaff, who despite his aristocratic birth, moves freely as a guest at the tables of middle-class society, Fenton is not acceptable to them.

'He doth object I am too great of birth'

says Fenton, explaining Page's objection to him. And Page himself says of him,

'He is of too high a region; he knows too much.'

This is the typical middle-class attitude towards the courtier. Page has made his fortune by his own industry, he has no wish to ally his daughter with a bejewelled miniature by Nicholas Hillyard, nor to have his wealth squandered in courtly extravagances.

Class distinction, therefore, operates mainly between the courtiers and the merchants, rather than between the upper and middle-classes. We find that Falstaff is accepted as a co-equal until, of course, he shows himself as a seducer of respectable burghers' wives, and the Host of the Garter, who to-day would be considered of inferior class to a rich merchant or a local J.P., is treated as an equal by Shallow and Page.

Through these characters, each easily recognizable to the audience of the Globe, we see a fairly complete cross-section of Elizabethan society and of its outlook on life; a society which believed in industry, just as the feudal society, which preceded it, believed in power; a society which was comparatively free from class prejudices, but disdainful of the frivolous, extravagant mode of life to which many of the upper classes had descended.

There is, however, another aspect of this society we must take note of and give point to. The scene is laid not in London, which with Bristol and York was one of the few real towns, but in Windsor. Windsor, like Stratford, was a country town, and such towns were typical of Elizabethan England—an England which had not suffered from the industrialism of the eighteenth and nineteenth centuries. The traditions and customs, the fashions and sports of the medieval village still persisted. The streets were not built in neat uniform patterns. Gardens and orchards intervened between business and residential houses; the focal points of life were the old village inn—in this case the Garter—the Grammar School, the Guildhall and the Church. The Park of Windsor abutted, or rather intruded, into the town as if the great oaks of England were anxious to remind the citizens of their agricultural background. Only very gradually were these giants hewn down by the axe of a money conscious society, and the split between country and town became complete. We are constantly reminded in the text of this persistence of country life in the midst of the town. The imagery of the play is interwoven with country illusions—'Jack-a-lent', 'cried-game', 'when night dogs run, all sorts of deer are chased'.

The popular pastimes of the Pages and the Fords are hawking and greyhound racing: they propose taking a turn in the park before settling to dinner, Shallow and Falstaff are involved in a poaching argument—a reference which is popularly supposed to be autobiographical of the author himself. The final climax of the comedy is played to the mock accompaniment of 'urchins, ouphs, and fairies, green and white', and at the end the participants go home to laugh their 'sport o'er by a country fire'. Thus we have in this play a picture of the society, atmosphere and appearance of Elizabethan country-town life, as it emerged from the barbarous feudal world of famine, insurrections and wars, whilst still retaining many of the picturesque habits and pastimes, as well as the physical appearance of medieval England.

The mixture of country and town, the pride of the new middle class, of the merchants and professional men, has been incorporated into the designer's scheme for this production. Thus the designer has made a point of contrasting the sensible broadcloth of the Pages and the Fords with the satins and laces of Fenton, and of providing a setting which hints at the mixture of parkland and town.

Comedy or Farce

There is one further production problem which I want to answer before proceeding to the more detailed problems of acting the play. Is this play a wild farce or a broad comedy? Ellen Terry in her memoirs recalls how Beerbohm Tree played it in farcical vein and was roundly trounced by some of the critics. In 1929 Oscar Asche presented the play in modern dress with telephones, cocktails and golf-clubs and Anne Page riding pillion on the back of Fenton's motor cycle. He even found it necessary to invent humour by altering such lines as 'smell like Bucklersbury in simple time' to 'smell like Piccadilly at closing time'. This production received for the most part the criticism it deserved. Again in 1935 Komisarjevsky turned the play into an extravaganza, in which Ford's soliloquies were punctuated by orchestral chords and Anne Page waltzed to Strauss. Our production will not be so presented. We will endeavour to extract the comedy from the situations that Shakespeare has written and to eschew cheap laughter at the expense of the play's atmosphere and realism. I have, I think, good reason for insisting on a realistic interpretation, since this is our Festival play and there are some who would criticize the choice of so minor a play as *The Merry Wives of Windsor* for such an occasion. I would like to justify it by showing the English humour of the play—the merry England which has played so large a part in the building of our institutions and national character.

The Situations

The play has other problems that must be answered, problems that may well arise from the fact that it was written in haste. I turn again to Johnson's criticism: '. . . The conduct of this drama is deficient; the action begins and ends often, before the conclusion, and the different parts might change places without inconvenience.' There is some truth in this. My reason for believing that the author was hurried in his work is based not on the situations, which are excessively funny, not on the characterizations, which are unusually brilliant, but on the fact that the action, as Johnson observes, 'begins and ends often' and 'the different parts might change places without inconvenience'. In other words the play tends to lack a cumulative effect and the situations often seem to end with a full stop. This gives it a jerkiness, causing it to lack flow in performance. Let me therefore examine these situations, so that we can see more clearly the pillars on which the framework of the comedy rests.

There are three main situations:

1. The Buck-Basket scene (Act III, Sc. 3).

2. The Fat Woman of Brentford (Act IV, Sc. 2).

3. The final mockery of Falstaff in Windsor Park (Act V, Sc. 5).

The difficulty is principally in situations 1 and 2, for the stuffing of the fat, old knight into a basket is of itself funnier than the beating he receives when he tries to escape in the disguise of the fat woman. Unless, however, the second situation succeeds in raising more laughter than the first and unless the expectation of comedy between these two scenes is strongly built up, we shall find that situation 2 is an anticlimax and it would have been better if Shakespeare had omitted it. Now the persons on whom the responsibility rests for maintaining the cumulative effect of comedy are Falstaff and Ford. It is on the success of the actors of these two parts in playing together, on their ability to act as a pair, that the comedy will depend. Falstaff by himself is not and cannot be the centrepiece of *The Merry Wives*, he relies on and requires the full co-operation of Ford. It is Ford's reactions to Falstaff's story of his escape in the buck-basket and his horror at hearing that yet another assignation has been arranged with his wife, that build up the expectation of comedy between the two seduction scenes. Thus, the Inn scene in which Ford, disguised as Brook, has his second interview with Falstaff (Act III, Sc. 5) assumes a special importance, and the comedy of this situation must be well stressed. In order to achieve the full comic effect of Falstaff's recital of his attempted seduction of Ford's wife, it is important that from the beginning of the play we treat Ford as somebody we laugh at, rather than somebody we sympathize with, and never for a moment must he be allowed to be a bore.

The last scene has its own peculiar comedy, concerned as it is with mock spooks and outlandishly disguised fairies. Here there is no danger of an anticlimax, so different is it in atmosphere and setting from the other two seduction scenes.

Besides these main situations there is a sub-plot, which resolves itself into the following:

1. The wooing of Anne Page by Slender.

2. The wooing of this eligible young lady by Caius, culminating in his ridiculous duel with Evans.

3. The wooing of Anne Page by Fenton, ending as all true comedy should end in the triumph of true love.

These three situations are neatly tied up in the final scene, and there is no problem here beyond the necessity of making Fenton and Anne very delightful young people; for their parts are of necessity somewhat pale beside those of Caius and Slender, and we must not allow our interest in them to be lost.

There is a further situation which presents a considerable problem: this is the revenge taken upon the Host of the Garter by Evans and Caius in the incident of the Germans' horses. (Act IV, Sc. 3, and the last eighteen lines of Act IV, Sc. 5.) Most critics of the play are agreed that this situation is faulty and probably results from a cut in the text. I have quite simply solved this difficulty by making a further cut and removing the situation entirely from the acting version. I will make no further excuse for doing so. I have taken a similar course with the catechizing of Page's son by Evans (Act IV, Sc. 1), which is no more than a contemporary comic interlude used as a stop-gap in the action. We have, therefore, one main problem so far as the cumulative nature of the play is concerned, and that is to ensure that the scenes of Falstaff's wooing do not tail off in expectation or in comedy.

The second problem which is the lack of flow of the action, due to the frequent changes of location and the numerous and rather isolated incidents, has set the designer and myself a problem. We have had to reconcile our desire to provide a setting realistic enough for a modern audience to recapture the flavour of Elizabethan life, a problem which did not exist for Shakespeare's audience, with our desire to give the play consistent flow. If we have erred in our solution on the side of too many changes of scene, I think we have rightly erred, having regard to the peculiar need for recapturing the flavour of the Elizabethan, domestic atmosphere.

Now we come to the requirements of characterization, many of which have been covered by previous remarks, though something yet remains to be said. In general we should observe with Johnson that despite its faults 'This comedy is remarkable for the variety and number of its personages who exhibit more characters appropriated and descriminated than perhaps can be found in any other play.' Ford, Page, their wives, Falstaff and his crew, Caius, Mistress Quickly, Evans, the Host, Slender and Shallow, are all complete, living persons about whom we can learn all there is to learn by a careful study of the text.

Mr. Justice Shallow and his cousin, Slender

First comes old Justice Shallow whom we have seen in an earlier play. Like Falstaff he seems to have lost something of his richness of character in his transition from the history plays, but he still remains the likeable, old bore, proud of his position as a Justice of the Peace and 'Coram', and anxious to impress upon the citizens of Windsor that he is no upstart merchant, but a gentleman born who writes himself 'Armigero' and displays a dozen white luces in his coat of arms. Shallow is a man of substance, owning his own deer park and keeper's lodge upon which property Falstaff and his crew have done violence. The old gentleman has journeyed up to Windsor from his home in Gloucestershire accompanied by his cousin, Slender, who is a material witness of Falstaff's crime. His purpose is to have the law on these poachers. He has already sent a present of venison to Master Page, an influential citizen, in order to procure his assistance. Page's qualities as an arbitrator, however, succeed in patching up the quarrel. And, to round matters off, Page readily agrees to Shallow's proposal, backed by Evans, of a match between Slender and Page's daughter.

Although the Shallow of *The Merry Wives* is less eccentric than the Shallow of *Henry IV*, he still preserves his old garrulous habits and his delight in tedious reminiscences. Once he gets hold of a subject it is very difficult to steer him off it, and it requires all the tact of Page to prevent the old man giving a personal demonstration of his powers as a fighter.

> 'Bodykins, Master Page, though I now be old, and of the peace, if I see a sword out, my finger itches to make one.'

He earns our sympathy in his fruitless attempt to instil a little common sense into the head of his cousin, Slender.

Like his elder relative, Cousin Slender is boastful of his family connexions, of his serving man and of his uncle's coat of arms. He shares with the old Justice of the Peace the same garrulous characteristics. But Slender is a victim to shyness, which is particularly frenzied when in the presence of an eligible young woman, or when any suggestions are made of his entering the matrimonial state. The first manifestations of his affliction are the usual ones of bashfulness; but bashfulness is quickly followed by a sudden loosening of his conversational powers which burst forth into a spate of uncontrolled chatter about a variety of inconsequential and irrelevant details.

This condition of shyness is by no means unusual. The shyest people are often the most uncontrolled chatterboxes, overwhelming their hearers with an odd assortment of subjects, which make conversation impossible. Thus it is that when invited to go into dinner, Slender chatters away about his serving man, his fencing encounter, his prowess at bear-baiting in a glorious mix up, which leaves poor Anne Page speechless. There is very little sign of manliness in this delightful creature. He is clearly susceptible to Anne's charms and follows his old tyrant of a cousin round Windsor bleating like a sentimental sheep for his 'sweet Anne Page'. Yet when the big moment of his life comes, when he is expected to declare his love for Anne and she asks him what his will is, off he goes on his senseless chattering:

'My will? Od's heartlings, that's a pretty jest indeed!
I ne'er made my will yet, I thank heaven; I'm not such
a sickly creature, I give heaven praise.'

Only at the end of the play do we see a little spark of spirit appear in him, when in a petulant outburst of impotent rage, he arrives wedded to a postmaster's boy.

'I came yonder at Eton to marry Mistress Anne Page, and
she's a great lubberly boy. If it had not been i' the church,
I would have swing'd him, or he should have swing'd me.
If I did not think it had been Anne Page, would I might
never stir! and 'tis a postmaster's boy.'

97

To sum up he is the embodiment of what the Elizabethans considered to be an ass: he cannot make love, he cannot hold his liquor, he boasts about his bravery, he whines about a hurt he got at fencing, and he is a thorough coward when a sword is drawn. Let me emphasize at once that he is not a pathetic character, but a nincompoop, and as such he is a fine comic characterization. Hazlitt says of him: 'He is a very potent piece of imbecility. In him the pretensions of the worthy Gloucester family are well kept up, and immortalized. He and his friend Sackerson, and his book of songs and his love of Anne Page and his having nothing to say to her can never be forgotten.'

The serving man of whom Slender is so proud is expressively called Simple, and evidently this is how Shakespeare intended him to be played. Like his master, he comes from Gloucestershire and is completely at a loss in the sophisticated life of Windsor with its proximity to the court. As a Gloucester man, he should be played with a local accent, for Shakespeare and Gloucestershire were neighbours and our author could not have resisted the fun of imitating the speech of a neighbouring county.

Sir Hugh Evans

Shallow and Slender are accompanied by Sir Hugh Evans who resembles all Shakespeare's schoolmasters in being both simple and pedantic. Of his other characteristics, we should note that he is also a parson and a Welshman. The parson side of Evans is, however, almost non-existent. He takes no part in the marriage ceremonies and his language seems hardly acceptable to any known religion; it has certainly no affinity to the usual conversation of a Christian priest. In brief we had better forget the parson side of Sir Hugh, as Shakespeare himself seems to have done. The important thing about Evans is that he is a Welshman, and to the Elizabethans a Welshman with his strange accent was always a figure of fun, far more than a Scotsman or an Irishman. Combine a Welshman with a pedant and you have the perfect recipe for a comedy character, and this is what Shakespeare has done for Sir Hugh. Like another Shakespeare schoolmaster, Holofernes by name, Evans is not only simple, by which I mean he is rather stupid, but he is also a toady. This sycophantic side of his character shows itself in his desire to curry favour with Shallow and Page, which results in his championship of Slender's cause against Dr. Caius. He is not, however, a complete coward and despite his natural misgivings at assuming the inappropriate role of a duellist, he displays a fiery determination to 'knog' Dr. Caius's 'urinals about his knave's costard'. In fact, Sir Hugh is a fiery little man who is, no doubt, a terror to his pupils, but who not unnaturally feels his knees wobbling a bit when he has a sword in his hand instead of a birch.

This duel between the two worthies was, of course, a particularly popular moment in the play to an Elizabethan audience; particularly to the swordsmen of the court, to whom nothing could be funnier than to see a doctor and a schoolmaster trying their inexpert hands at the art of fencing. It must have been something like the reactions of our football fans to a match between the French Medical Association and the Chapter of Westminster Abbey.

Dr. Caius

Sir Hugh Evans's redoubtable opponent, Dr. Caius, is another fiery little man as we see by his treatment of Simple, whom he finds hiding in his closet, and by his general behaviour to his domestics. Again Shakespeare is making use of an accent to accentuate comedy—in this case the equally laughable French accent. Moreover, he was probably insuring his success by caricaturing a notorious contemporary doctor. Such a joke is of no help to us to-day, but there is sufficient fun in Caius without it. It might be worth remembering, however, that Elizabethan doctors had a high opinion of Parisian medical knowledge and that a French accent, even if assumed, was considered a help to medical preferment, just as to-day we prefer a Gallicized chef. Like Evans, Caius is possessed of a fiery disposition. In this respect he is a complete contrast to the other unsuccessful wooer of Anne Page, Slender, for whereas the latter can only stamp petulantly when he finds himself fooled at the end, Caius runs off to 'raise all Windsor' for the trick played upon him.

I think we may imagine that this eccentric gentleman exists on a very high plane of nervous excitement, rather like a temperamental French conjuror. The Englishman's view of the excitable Frenchman has not changed much in the last four hundred years, and in presenting a doctor and a school-master Shakespeare was presenting two sure-fire comedy hits; by making one French and the other Welsh, he was enlarging the bull's eye.

Mistress Quickly and John Rugby

However much of a fire-eater and a quack Dr. Caius may be, he is nevertheless a successful man. His services are constantly in demand; he is off to the court when we first meet him, and he is considered a suitable suitor by Mrs. Page for her daughter's hand.

'The doctor is well money'd and his friends potent at court.' We must imagine, therefore, his household as a respectable, well-run affair. Mrs. Quickly and John Rugby must evidently be God-fearing persons, clean and sober, if they are to run his domestic affairs. This fact places an immediate gulf between the Mistress Quickly of this play with the hostess of *Henry IV, Part I*, who is married to the host of the Boar's Head, or, indeed, the Mistress Quickly of *Henry IV, Part II*, who is a poor widow of Eastcheap, or with the wife of Pistol in *Henry V* who dies of a 'malady of France'; but to worry our heads, about the inconsistencies of these Eastcheap characters is not part of our job. We must play what is written in the text of *The Merry Wives* and not waste our time casting our eyes over our shoulders at other plays in which characters bearing the same names occur.

Although Mrs. Quickly is an efficient housekeeper, this does not prevent her from being an incurable matchmaker, and from turning a pretty, if not particularly honest, penny from the secondary profession of a go-between. She is clearly lacking in principle and a gay bird, as is testified by Pistol:

'This punk is one of cupid's carriers.'

She has an eye for a good jest, enjoying her employment as a go-between by the fat knight, no less than her ridiculous masquerade as an outsize fairy.

John Rugby, whom she keeps well under her thumb, is probably an apprentice to the doctor, rather than a serving man. The fact that he is addressed as John Rugby, as opposed to the more simple John or Rugby, indicates that he is of some birth. He is probably the son of a burgher of Windsor and will eventually graduate to a doctor in his turn. He seems to have a predeliction for praying and indeed in the high-powered life of the Caius-Quickly household, he may have good reasons for it.

The Pages and the Fords

I will now turn to two more households, those of the Pages and the Fords. Page and Ford are written as strong contrasting types. The former is tolerant, jovial and hospitable, a peace-maker and an easy-going husband. The latter is jealous, irascible and supremely confident of his own cunning. Both are well-to-do and occupy respectable positions in the life of the country-town. Their relations with each other are strengthened by the intimacy between their wives, but in other respects they are mutually averse to each other's temperament. Besides the characteristics we have already mentioned, Page is obviously a keen sportsman with his greyhound and his hawks 'for the bush'; he is also a good family man and keen to obtain a rich suitor for his daughter's hand, though he loses our respect by his use of a low piece of cunning in order to insure the success of his candidate. The trick he plays on his daughter shows him to be a trifle insensitive, for he is prepared to sacrifice his daughter's happiness to increase his family fortune. There is a point where the bluffness of a John Bull ceases to be a virtue, and Page is a typical John Bull.

This lack of sensitivity to the question of her daughter's happiness is shared by his wife, Mistress Page, who champions Dr. Caius. But the battle between husband and wife over the question of Anne's husband brings out two points relative to their characters. The first is that Mistress Page is an independent and emancipated lady, who is quite prepared to stand up to the head of the household and to face the consequences.

The second is that in their choice of suitors they display a difference of outlook. Though both are primarily interested in the financial side of the affair, Mistress Page chooses Caius for his interest at court, whereas Page deliberately discards Fenton for that very reason. Although she is a stout supporter of the material outlook of the middle-class, Mistress Page does not share her husband's dislike for the court; she is even willing to consider Fenton's appeal to her, though she ultimately decides against him. Clearly she and Mistress Ford are flattered by the winks and oglings of the courtiers from Windsor Castle, though they desire more solid gains when it comes to the question of matrimony. But Mistress Page bears no ill will for Fenton's success, and at the end she displays her fundamental good humour by wishing Master Fenton 'many, many merry days', and advocating that the whole company, 'Sir John and all', go home to laugh the 'sport o'er by a country fire'.

Of the two good gossips, Mistress Ford is the more daring in her approach to her suitors. It is she who entertains Falstaff at her house, and although we are persuaded of her chaste intentions on this occasion, we could not be equally sanguine were the suitor to be younger and better favoured. Mistress Quickly, who knows her well, says to Sir John:

> 'The best courtier of them all, when the court lay at Windsor, could never have brought her to such a canary.'

And if this be exaggeration there is also her husband's jealousy, for which he probably has some grounds. Moreover, she seems fairly expert in arranging suitable times and places for clandestine meetings and for deceiving her husband when he arrives unexpectedly. I fear the old dodge of inviting a gentleman to come and see the picture 'that you wot of', when her husband is away, has been used before. So that I wonder if the attentions of the earls and pensioners mentioned by Mistress Quickly were treated so indifferently. But then, by way of excuse, we realize that 'she leads a very frampold life', with such a suspicious creature for a husband, for she is by nature a warm-blooded and merry lady.

Merriness is, of course, the main characteristic of both the

Windsor wives. Life is good, money is plentiful, servants are obedient; both ladies are newly emancipated from the medieval subjugation of wives; there is ample food in the larder and fine linen in the cupboards and they are possessed with abundant humour and high spirits. Of the two, Mistress Page has the more fertile brain for a jest, and Mistress Ford the more adventurous spirit in carrying it out. After all, husbands must learn their place and the merry wives of Windsor will not be put down by jealousy, nor by having their views on their daughters' marriage crossed.

Anne Page and Fenton

In contrast to these mature characters stands 'sweet Anne Page', of whom our only criticism is that we don't see enough of her. As the daughter of a good middle-class family, she is simply dressed and well mannered, but she is clearly no pawn to be pushed around by her parents in order to increase their wealth. Anne has a mind of her own and a determined will to get what she wants. She is in love with Fenton, and if 'humblest suit cannot attain' her father's consent, 'why then—hark you hither', and this 'hark you hither' is none other than a plan for elopement in face of her parents' obstinacy. She, too, is of a merry disposition and enjoys to the full Slender's inept attempts to woo her. She had rather be 'set quick i' the earth and bowl'd to death with turnips' than marry him. On the other hand her spirit shows itself not only in her elopement, but by her careful proving of Fenton's motives before consenting to run away with him.

We have already spoken of Fenton's interest in Page's wealth, but it is clear that pecuniary motives are secondary to his love for Anne once he has come to know this charming young lady. He declares that he finds her 'of more value than stamps in gold or sums in sealed bags', and this is proved by his elopement, which would effectively bar him from participating in the family fortune. He is of a generous, warm-hearted nature and, although Mistress Quickly realizes that her financial advantage lies with the other suitors, she is strongly inclined towards Fenton:

'a kind heart he hath: a woman would run through fire
for such a kind heart.'

Despite the fact that she is torn in two between Fenton's kind
heart and the gold that would come her way if she were able
to make a match with Slender or with Caius, she will do what
she can 'but speciously for Master Fenton'.

Mine Host of the Garter

The chances of Fenton's success are principally championed
by the Host of the Garter who, as a man of wide experience,
knows well enough that a high-spirited young man 'who
capers and dances and speaks holiday' will 'carry it' over his
more eligible, but less attractive, rivals. As proprietor of the
Garter Inn, which is, as we have already said, one of the focal
points of the citizens' lives, the Host is a man of considerable
influence in Windsor. Moreover, the proximity of the castle
gives extra importance to him and to his hostelry. Queen
Elizabeth was in the habit of entertaining foreign embassies at
her Castle of Windsor. Lavish as the Queen might be in the
matter of her private wardrobe, she was thoroughly parsi-
monious with her public purse, and the large retinues that
accompanied the ambassadors were often forced to seek accom-
modation outside the royal castle; that meant they had to put
up at the local hostelry. These visitations from foreigners, not
only taught the Host much about life as a whole, giving him an
easy tolerant view of the ways of human beings, they also brought
him riches and a reputation for astuteness in business matters.
The foreigners and courtiers who frequent his inn have,
moreover, had a marked influence on his manner of speaking.
His outlandish expressions are borrowed from his strange
guests or from the slang of the court. Much of the spice of the
Host's talk is lost to us to-day since, like Caius, he was probably
a caricature of a contemporary figure; as such he was highly
amusing to Elizabethan audiences and his character was imi-
tated in at least two other plays of the period.

He is, of course, a broad, big man and like many big men
he has a highly developed sense of fun. It is he who arranges

the mock duel between Evans and Caius, and his reason for doing so is because it will be a good jest. We know this incident will later lose nothing in the telling over a good jug of ale. This big broad man has a sense of fair play as well as a sense of fun and he champions the cause of Fenton and Anne, arranging their marriage for them.

Falstaff

His guests at the inn are of course our old friends from Eastcheap, Sir John and his ruffianly companions, not forgetting his page, Robin. We have already discussed the transformation of Sir John from the histories to *The Merry Wives* and have seen that we would be wise to base his character on what is written about him in this play without troubling our heads about his past. We know that Elizabeth wanted to see Sir John in love, and that meant that she wanted to be made merry by seeing the old knight put down by the gentler sex. Perhaps she thought it was time to put an end to such a rascal, and being a thorough believer in her own sex, she considered that women were the best people to put him down. So put down he must be as sure as his guts are made of puddings.

There is, of course, no hint of genuine affection in his wooing of the wives. It is purely a matter of lechery mixed with greed for their husbands' angels. If Mine Host of the Garter is a big man, Sir John is, as we know, bigger. His size is important not only for the comedy of the basket scene, but also for the comedy of the fat woman of Brentford. When the Elizabethans talked of a fat man they meant a very fat man, a proud product of roast beef and hodge pudding and gallons of ale—a 'whale with so many tuns of oil in his belly' as Mistress Ford puts it. To see this monster frisking about with the gait and mannerisms of a lover was, and is to-day, the main fun of the play. But despite the fact that Sir John of *The Merry Wives* is a dupe almost throughout, there are snatches of cunning about the old rascal which show that his spirit is not quite dead, and that, when not a victim to Cupid's arrow, he can score off the lot of them. Thus he puts down Simple and magnificently turns the tables on the whole mockery of the fairies, by asserting with true Falstaffian bravado that he knew all the time they were not real.

Pistol, Nym, Bardolph and Robin

His companions have changed very little, or not at all, from the earlier plays. Pistol remains the same braggart as he appears in *Henry V*, and Johnson says of him that he is 'the model of all bullies that have yet appeared on the English stage'. Nym, too, is unchanged and still displays the same idiosyncrasies and the same absurd use of the word 'humour' which he has of course picked up from the fashionable pedantry of the time. Bardolph is the oldest and most loyal of Sir John's retainers, and in many ways, despite his disgraceful end in *Henry V*, the most honest. He, at least, has the merit of seeking honest service when he is dismissed, and is unaware of the stratagems of Pistol and Nym to rouse the anger of Ford and Page against his master.

Robin may or may not be the same page as appears in *Henry IV, Part II*, and the boy of *Henry V*. At all events in this play we see him as an industrious servant to Sir John until he is taken up by the Page household when, bribed by good clothes and adequate food, he does not scruple to take part in the trick that is being played on his old master. He is, in fact, a typical boy, who loves good fun as well as another and has no scruples when it comes to loyalty, having never known what honest living is.

Ford and Master Brook

We have strayed a little from the Page and Ford families and we must now return to Mr. Ford, who weighs the balance of the comedy in the scales with Falstaff. Ford is the jealous husband, and the jealous husband in a domestic play is a matter for laughter rather than tears. The comedy of his character is, of course, enhanced by his complete lack of humour and his enormous conceit. Ford had, as we have already said, probably some grounds for suspecting that his wife might play him false. Mistress Ford was a pretty woman, in fact she was probably the handsomer of the two wives, and to have a pretty wife living in proximity to the gentlemen of the court was a tricky affair. A jealous husband in an Elizabethan or indeed a Restoration comedy was nearly always an occasion for comedy. The 'cuckold' theme was exceedingly popular, and the mere mention of the word was enough to bring down the house and stamp the character as a butt for ridicule.

Ford makes the mistake of taking himself too seriously and of thinking himself too clever. His feelings of bitter anguish when, disguised as Brook, he hears from Falstaff of the assignations of his wife are understandable enough, but his crowing over Page's tolerance requires that he, like Falstaff, must be put down. His rash and ridiculous action of promoting his wife's assignation with his rival and then bursting in upon her with a crowd of his fellow citizens shows his impulsive and thoughtless character; such indifference to his wife's good name is inexcusable, and if we are not to hate him, which is against the harmony of comedy, we must be allowed to laugh at him.

We may consider what sort of disguise would be assumed by this foolish cuckold when he visits Falstaff. We can hardly believe that it is a very good disguise, for Ford is too impulsive to carry through a design with any kind of efficiency. He must, of course, give the impression of being very rich in order to engage Falstaff's interest. So we will have him dressed up as courtier with rings and ruffles and feathers, with perhaps a rapier or tall stick which will embarrass his movement, for Ford is unused to managing such properties. We imagine, too, that nothing fits very well, for part of the comedy of action between him and Falstaff must lie in the actor's play with his unaccustomed disguise. Falstaff will of course be aware of a certain incongruity in the dress and behaviour of his visitor, but he will be blinded by his wealth and his own lecherous desires. Ford's airs as Master Brook, the rich gentleman, are in keeping with his stilted form of speech:

> '. . . not to charge you; for I must let you understand I think myself in better plight for a lender than you are: the which hath something emboldened me to this unseasoned intrusion.'

Such language demands a rather poor attempt at a grand

manner of speech and deportment. He should perhaps be troubled with a false moustache or wig and his face should reveal his anxiety, lest the whole unaccustomed disguise should fall down about his knees.

Ford is a conceited man, despising such 'secure' fools as Page and priding himself on his cleverness in probing his wife's honesty. He is effectively made a fool of by his wife, indeed that high spirited lady and her gossip, Mistress Page, would not lose such a chance of putting down a jealous husband and of asserting their independence. Nevertheless, he has the grace to acknowledge his error handsomely and to ask her pardon:

> 'Pardon me, wife. Henceforth do what thou wilt;
> I rather will suspect the sun with cold
> Than thee with wantonness: now doth thy honour stand,
> In him that was of late an heretic,
> As firm as faith.'

Thus he is cured, and we must believe in his sincerity and firm determination to mend his ways. As the reconciled husband he is allowed to bring about the final reconciliation of all the parties:

> 'All parties pleased, now let us in to feast,
> And laugh at Slender, and the doctor's jest.
> He hath got the maiden, each of you a boy
> To wait upon you, so God give you joy:
> And Sir John Falstaff, now shall you keep your word
> For Brook this night shall lie with Mistress Ford.'

I prefer the final lines from the First Quarto edition together with the penultimate gem of Evans:

> 'I will also dance and eat plums at your wedding.'

though for the rest of the last scene we will follow the Folio text.

This last scene has its own special magic, for although these fairies and hobgoblins are but the children of the town companioned by Pistol, Mistress Quickly and Sir Hugh Evans, yet the oak of Herne the hunter is a mysterious place for a rendezvous when 'the Windsor bell hath struck twelve'.

And so they go out of the forest of Windsor, leaving it silent and alone in the moonlight, a prey to the real fairies who inhabit it, or to the ghostly ministrations of Herne the hunter. Meantime the prosperous little country-town of Windsor shuts its shutters and goes to bed.

POSTSCRIPT

One of the difficulties of producing a comedy of situation such as *The Merry Wives* is that, in rehearsing it, there is no yard-stick to measure the audience's laughter. What provokes laughter in the theatre is the sense of the ridiculous, but what appears ridiculous to the actors will often provoke no reaction from the audience. When we started rehearsing this play we knew that the situations had to make the audience laugh; if we failed to do this, the play would fall flat, for it has no other purpose.

Our rehearsals began in high spirits, but we realized soon enough that what we were laughing at was ourselves and not at Falstaff or Ford or Caius or Evans. All of us were aware of the deception of laughing at the play in rehearsal. It is a strong superstition of the stage that what causes laughter in rehearsal will fail to do so before an audience. We struggled painfully to infuse comedy into the situation of the buck-basket, the fat woman, Brook's disguise, the duel and the mock-fairies' gambols. Yet, try as we might to think up comic business and to invent preposterous mishaps, the scenes remained singularly flat. Not only were the timing and emphasis lost by such tricks, but the text was unyielding to our efforts, and provided no sort of cover for our clowning. We burst ourselves in our efforts to squeeze comic business into the restricted material of the scenes, but each rehearsal ended with a feeling of despair, together with a load of curses on the author for his seemingly maladroit text. When all further effort was in vain, we held a word rehearsal, leaving out all our laboriously rehearsed effects, and lo and behold, the comedy was born.

This overloading of comedy in rehearsal is perhaps an

inevitable process in arriving at a true rendering of it. Since comedy arises from understatement rather than overstatement, it seems that we must first overstate it, before we know what to discard. We forget, too, that we must first establish the reality, before we can establish the ridiculous. True ridicule is achieved by confronting real people with an unfamiliar situation. The stuffing of Falstaff into a basket of dirty clothes is only funny if Falstaff is a real person and not a caricature. If a producer is faced with making an audience laugh, his first task must be to insist on the reality of characterization. However much the actor may desire to invent comic business, he must at all costs be curbed from fixing this business until he has found the reality of his character. This is more difficult than it sounds, for the actor, who is ultimately responsible for the audience's laughter, will easily lose confidence if he sees no help forthcoming from the producer. There is no easy answer to this problem of confidence between producer and actor. Sometimes it may be necessary for the producer to invent comic business that he knows full well he will later discard, in order to keep the actor's confidence. The confidence of the actor, however it is achieved, is immeasurably important, and never more so than in comedy, for success will only be won if the actor is sure of his laughs.

Once reality of characterization has been achieved, the actor can be trusted to try out his comic business for himself and, even if he pushes his invention too far in early rehearsal, his own sense of what is right or wrong for the truth of his characterization will quickly redress the balance in the light of this inner knowledge. But comedy will inevitably degenerate into caricature or burlesque unless the foundations of truthful characterization have first been securely laid.

ROMEO AND JULIET

ROMEO AND JULIET
Assembly Hall, Edinburgh
1st September 1952

Old Vic Theatre
15th September 1952

CHORUS	WILLIAM DEVLIN
SAMPSON	WOLFE MORRIS
GREGORY	GEORGE MURCELL
ABRAHAM	HUGH DAVID
BALTHASAR	JOHN BRESLIN
TYBALT	LAURENCE PAYNE
BENVOLIO	WILLIAM SQUIRE
MONTAGUE	RUPERT HARVEY
LADY MONTAGUE	DAPHNE HEARD
CAPULET	JOHN PHILLIPS
LADY CAPULET	YVONNE COULETTE
ESCALUS, *Prince of Verona*	WILLIAM DEVLIN
MERCUTIO	PETER FINCH
PARIS	JOHN WARNER
ROMEO	ALAN BADEL
PETER	NEWTON BLICK
NURSE	ATHENE SEYLER
JULIET	CLAIRE BLOOM
OLD CAPULET	ROBERT WELLES
FRIAR LAURENCE	LEWIS CASSON
APOTHECARY	WOLFE MORRIS
FRIAR JOHN	ROBERT WELLES
PAGE TO PARIS	ALAN DOBIE

OFFICERS, CITIZENS, SERVANTS, MUSICIANS AND LADIES:
JOHN BRESLIN, HUGH DAVID, CHURTON FAIRMAN,
BERNARD KILBY, JAMES MAXWELL, DONALD PICKERING,
DOUGLAS RAIN, DENIS RAYMOND, LLOYD RECKORD,
BRUCE SHARMAN, ERIC THOMPSON, BARBARA GRIMES,
PHYLLIDA LAW, ANDREE MELLY.

Sets and Costumes by Roger Furse.
Music composed by Clifton Parker.

Here is the Nanny of all time

JULIET: Claire Bloom   NURSE: Athene Seyler

'Which are the children of an idle brain'

MERCUTIO: Peter Finch

The character of Juliet cannot be acted, it must be lived

JULIET: Claire Bloom

ROMEO AND JULIET

L IKE *Love's Labour's Lost* this is a young play, written when
the playwright was between twenty-five and thirty. Chrono-
logically, it is considered by Sir Edmund Chambers to be later
than *Love's Labour's Lost* and earlier than *A Midsummer Night's
Dream.* As an early play it displays a certain weakness, characteristic of this lyrical period of the poet's life—his irresistible
urge to concern himself with puns and conceits of language.
This punning and word-play can be an embarrassment to us
to-day, who have lost the humour and the ear for such matters,
more especially so when the young word-spinner's ebullience
allows it to burst forth in tragic passages, such as the play on
the word 'Ay' in Juliet's outburst of grief, and in the passage
between Peter and the musicians. In general, however, such
outbursts of word-music can be accepted by us and woven
into the lyrical framework of the tragedy; for the first important point to remember about *Romeo and Juliet* is that it is a
lyrical play.

To point the importance that word-music plays in *Romeo
and Juliet,* we have only to look at the moon-drenched duet
of the balcony meeting, the torchlight aria of the Queen Mab
speech, the dawn cadenza of the farewell scene, the ghost
sonata of Juliet's potion speech, and Romeo's final swan-song
in the tomb:

'How oft when men are at the point of death
Have they been merry! Which their keepers call

A lightening before death: O how may I
Call this a lightening? O my love! my wife!
Death, that hath sucked the honey of thy breath
Hath had no power yet upon thy beauty:
Thou art not conquer'd; beauty's ensign yet
Is crimson in thy lips and in thy cheeks,
And death's pale flag is not advanced there.'

Such passages of word-music are, if you like, a play upon words, a mixture of metaphors, a conceit of imagery—but they are also word-magic, spun by a master weaver of language; by a playwright who knew how words, when used with inspiration, charged with emotion and shot through with lyrical magic, can produce the same effect as can the sound of viols, hautboys ánd all the consort of heavenly instruments that hale men's souls out of their bodies.

To reconcile this elaboration of language with the tragic content of *Romeo and Juliet*, we must first recognize that this musical language is a part of the play, as important as is the score of an opera. To try to damp down the lyrical effect produced by the word-music is to destroy the magic of the play.

There are other signs of youthful workmanship; notably the lengthy winding up of the plot in the last scene. This we will deal with drastically, for we must bear in mind that our audience lack the endurance which must have characterized the spectators of the Globe, and three and a half hours on a hard bench in the Assembly Hall, Edinburgh, is not conducive to successful entertainment. We must, therefore, pledge ourselves not to exceed the Chorus's statement, 'the two-hours' passage of our stage'—an exaggeration by any standards of speed—by more than one hour, no matter what the sacrifices may mean. To keep the play within its time limit, let us bear in mind that modern acting has developed a tendency to stress effects of tension by using elaborate pauses. Such pauses can, of course, be enormously effective in Shakespeare's plays as in others, but in so far as they destroy or break the flow of words, which makes the music of the play, they are harmful. The effect of speed in the delivery of Shakespeare's lines—the

116

speaking of lines 'trippingly on the tongue'—is too often neglected, because it is hard to master; John Gielgud is a notable exception to this. When used in the right places, speed is of considerable importance. We are too apt to linger over our parts, savouring their meaning at the expense of the movement of the play. In studying the play, we must pay particular attention to pace and tempo generally, for it is by the correct use of tempo, be it slow or fast, that the word-music is controlled.

Now for the play itself and its treatment. It is called in the First Quarto, 'An excellent conceited Tragedie of *Romeo and Juliet*', but we would do well to study the Prologue to the play for a further insight into what the playwright had in mind.

'Two households, both alike in dignity,
(In fair Verona, where we lay our scene)
From ancient grudge break to new mutiny,
Where civil blood makes civil hands unclean.
From forth the fatal loins of these two foes
A pair of star-crossed lovers take their life;
Whose misadventured, piteous overthrows
Do with their death bury their parents' strife.
The fearful passage of their death-marked love,
And the continuance of their parents' rage,
Which, but their children's end, nought could remove,
Is now the two hours' passage of our stage.'

I would ask you to consider for a moment certain key passages of this Prologue: first, 'Two households, both alike in dignity . . . from ancient grudge break to new mutiny.'

We are in Verona in the fifteenth century. Perhaps Verona is a little like London in the last years of the sixteenth century; these matters of location and period are supremely unimportant to the placeless and timeless flight of Shakespeare's imagination. Though his scenes be laid in Greece, Rome or Egypt, his period be pre-historic or fifteenth century, yet the life that is breathed into his characters is drawn from the living, contemporary existence of his own age. That is the strength of his characterization.

We are, then, in Shakespeare's Verona, sun-baked with a

heat that makes men quick to strike 'being moved'. The sort of drenching heat in which gallants and their minions lounge the street, idly exchanging quips, as they sprawl against corner-posts, mocking at passers-by, especially if they happen to be ancient ladies coquetting behind their fans. The sort of heat that breeds mischief and flies. In this proud city-state of Verona live the two great families of Montague and Capulet, proud of their nobility, jealous of their prerogatives, marrying their daughters and sons with careful attention to the wealth and stability of their houses. Between these two clans exists a bitter and continual blood-feud, the origin of which is un-explained and is for our purposes unimportant. It springs from the inevitable rivalry of two households, neither of which can bear to be outdone in precedence or wealth by the other. This rivalry, fanned by the sort of swordsman-braggart that each family cultivates, set in the quarrelsome heat of the piazzas of Verona and framed by the code of honour of a duelling age, when to study the changing fashions of swordsmanship and to draw blood are the necessary stigmata of manhood, is bound to present a serious problem to the upholders of law and order. In this struggle for family power, not only the noble members of the households are affected, but the quarrel lies no less deeply between the serving men. Sampson and Gregory delib-erately set upon Abraham and Balthasar in the first scene of the play when they see Tybalt approaching, knowing that this will draw the commendations of their fire-eating lord.

No matter what severity the energy and civic sense of the ruling prince may display, it appears impossible, short of a general purge, to extirpate the evils of these constantly re-curring brawls, which cause such damage to the citizens and bring such shame on the city. This is Verona, not unlike London within the living memory of Shakespeare and his contemporaries where the great noble houses still remembered their wounds from the Wars of the Roses and where, even in Shakespeare's day, the citizens could be alarmed by the call of 'An Essex' or 'A Leicester'.

Let us again return to our Prologue: 'From forth the fatal loins of these two foes, a pair of star-crossed lovers take their

life . . . The fearful passage of their death-marked love . . .'
These latter words raise the question of the part that destiny
plays in this tragedy. In most of the great Shakespeare tragedies,
particularly in the more mature works—*Lear, Timon, Othello*
and *Antony*—fate, as it is understood by the Greek dramatists,
plays no important part in the punishment or purgation of the
heroes and heroines. Even in *Macbeth* and *Hamlet* it is the sin,
or the will, of the leading characters, rather than the prophecies
of Witches or the invocation of a Ghost, that bring about the
tragedy. Shakespeare seems to have rejected any thought of
predestination and, although he lays great store by super-
natural warnings, he does not accept the philosophy of inter-
vention by Divine power to order men's actions. Man creates
his own destiny and as he sows, so must he reap. Lear and
Timon, Macbeth and his wife, Antony and Cleopatra,
Hamlet, Coriolanus, Othello, the Richards, all meet the ends
that they themselves have prepared by their temperaments
and deeds—be it their jealousy, their pride, their folly or their
weakness. But here, in this first major tragedy that Shakespeare
wrote, we find in 'the fatal passage of their death-marked love'
an inevitable destiny surrounding the two lovers. Antony and
Cleopatra were also involved in such a death-marked love,
but Antony and Cleopatra were mature, experienced lovers;
moreover, their union was by man's standards immoral, and,
therefore, in the eyes of the audience, punishable. Romeo and
Juliet are children—the one scarcely a man, the other a mere
girl of fourteen. Their love is essentially pure and indeed in
its social implication of uniting the two rival families, a thing
to be desired by Christian principles. It may be argued that
their love was 'too rash, too unadvis'd, too sudden', but the
audience, which is the judge of the play's morality, will
inevitably side with these young people. Moreover, their union
is encouraged by older and wiser people in the persons of the
Nurse and the Friar.

But yet we would be wrong to jump to the conclusion that
in this single instance the playwright has been untrue to his
belief in man's ultimate power to control his destiny, and to
conclude that fate has intervened to strike down these young

people in the same way as it does in the novels of Thomas Hardy or in the early Greek tragedies. The guilty parties are present in this as in all Shakespeare's plays, though they are not the so-called principal characters. The motivators of this 'excellent conceited tragedie' are neither Romeo and Juliet nor fate, but the 'two households both alike in dignity', with which words the Prologue opens the play. The Capulets and Montagues are the cause of their children's death-marked love. It is their family quarrel, their stupid pride, their mistaken sense of honour which causes the 'misadventured, piteous over-throws' of the star-crossed lovers.

Now in this, as in all things concerned with the treatment of the play, we must preserve a sense of balance. It does not mean, as I believe Bernard Shaw is reported to have said to a young producer who was preparing a production of the play, that the only thing that matters is the fights. The fights are important, for they are the outward expression of the forces which control the destiny of the lovers, but those forces, themselves, are important too. The sense of pride, the misplaced honour, the hot-blooded, callous attitude of the members of the two households and their servants must be given due value in the balancing of the production. In this matter we shall have more to say when we consider the characterization. But there is another matter, about which Shaw did not speak, and that is the lyrical side of the play which springs from the central characters themselves. The households are important as the motivators of the tragedy and their rivalry is the frame-work inside which, and because of which, the tragedy happens, but the centre of the tragedy is the love story of Romeo and Juliet which, flourishing like the flower upon the manure heap, is all the more lovely because of the foulness that surrounds it.

'Which, but their children's end, nought could remove.' Here is the eventual purgation of the tragedy. This evil which lies heavily upon the city-state of Verona can only be purged one way; by the cruel extermination of the most worth-while fruit of the houses themselves. Nothing short of the deaths of Romeo and Juliet could have brought home to the principal sinners the enormity of their crime. Only the extermination of the first-born opened the door of Egypt to the Israelites. The sight of these two favourite children, who defied their parents' rage, purges the hatred—blood-stained hand is stretched to blood-stained hand and both wiped clean with tears.

Capulet

Let us now look at the characters themselves; firstly, the family of the Capulets. The head of the household, Capulet, is a man of some maturity. He is considerably older than his wife, who clearly regards him as a meddling old fool. At all events, he has passed his dancing days for it is thirty years since he took part in a mask'd dance. We may put him between fifty and sixty. His age has put him beyond the days when a father can easily understand the mentality of a fourteen-year-old daughter. His life, however, has not been an austere one, he has 'been a mouse-hunt in his time', and even now he clearly enjoys a frolic with the 'fresh, female buds' that attend his feast. His description of the scene to Paris is a clear indication of his own delight in revelling:

'At my poor house look to behold this night
Earth-treading stars that make dark heaven light—
Such comfort as do lusty young men feel
When well-apparell'd April on the heel
Of limping winter treads, even such delight
Among fresh female buds shall you this night
Inherit at my house . . .'

And again, what could be more indicative of an elderly beau, who has not lost his taste for quizzing the girls, than his delightful:

'Ah ha, my mistresses! Which of you all
Will now deny to dance? She that makes dainty.
She, I'll swear, hath corns. Am I come near ye now?'

Capulet then, for all his sense of honour and dignity, is no morose father. He has a taste for a party. He enjoys the preparations for his daughter's wedding—in playing the role of housewife—in caring for the baked meats and in supervising the servants. In fact, he becomes young again when the candles are lit, the tables spread and the fiddles tuning up.

> 'This night I hold an old accustom'd feast,
> Whereto I have invited many a guest,
> Such as I love . . .'

Once the merriment has started and the wine is passed round, he easily forgets his family feud, and he will not be put out by Tybalt, when this quarrelsome fellow tries to spoil the fun by pointing out that one of the masked guests is none other than the son of the hated Montague family. His natural hospitality and love of good cheer overcome any artificial prejudices on such an occasion, and he roundly chides his fire-eating nephew for desiring to drive Romeo out.

All this is the pleasanter side of Capulet's character, but unfortunately the endearing generosity which he shows to his guests is not so visible within the circle of his family. To his wife, his daughter and her Nurse, he is a tetchy and tyrannical father, who considers himself to have the right to dispose of them as he wishes and to order all things in the household. Once the door is closed on his guests his word is law and little time is spent on considering the inclinations of his family. He decides upon his daughter's bridegroom without regard for her feelings. But however arbitrary we may consider such arrangements to-day, we must not overstress their importance, remembering that the fixing of marriages was a common part of the social structure of Shakespeare's day. After all, however little prudence he shows in refusing to listen to his daughter's pleading against the intended match with Paris, we must not forget that his desire to hasten this match was largely due to a misunderstanding of the cause of Juliet's grief. He jumps to the conclusion that Juliet is weeping for Tybalt, and it is because he 'counts it dangerous that she doth give her sorrow so much sway' that Capulet insists on an early marriage with Paris, 'to stop the inundation of her tears'. In any case it is surely more the duty of the mother than of the father to know the daughter's heart.

Lady Capulet

Here, however, we find one of the main causes of the tragedy. Lady Capulet has never possessed the key to Juliet's heart, nor has she tried to do so. She is not an unnatural mother; she can feel grief for her daughter's death, but to a greater degree than her husband, she is blinded by the senseless pride of her family. Lady Capulet is younger than her husband. We know that she was a mother at fourteen or thereabouts, and even allowing for one or two other children, since deceased, she cannot be more than thirty-five or so. We imagine her to be still beautiful, and, although there is no direct evidence of it, we can imagine that her life is not fulfilled by her elderly husband. The difference of years between the two has inclined her to look elsewhere for an outlet, which she finds in the rigid maintenance of the dignity and rank of the Capulet family, making up in pride what her husband lacks in this respect. She despises her husband, considering him more fit to bear a crutch than a sword, but she will maintain his position and rank in the household. Those lines, in my view wrongly ascribed to the Nurse in Act IV, Sc. 4:

'Go, you cot-quean, go,
   Get you to bed, faith, you'll be sick to-morrow
For this night's watching.'

indicate her general feeling of contempt for this elderly husband. No doubt she has had her troubles with him. No doubt this mouse-hunting husband has been the cause of much distress to the wife, but her nature has been soured by one reason or another, and we must feel little sympathy for this proud Italian matron whose outburst of grief and venomous hatred over Tybalt's murder is largely influenced by the loss of a supporter of her family's honour, and who is deaf to considerations of justice. Tybalt is perhaps the person in whom Lady Capulet is most interested, but we have no evidence other than surmise based on her attitude to life. As for her daughter's supposed death, we must believe her grief to be genuine, but this grief is also tinged with, what for her, is a major tragedy, the loss of a splendid match between her household and the Prince's kinsman, Paris. The character of Lady Capulet is not intended to draw sympathy; it must not do so. It is strong and eminently actable.

Tybalt

An equally unsympathetic and equally actable character is her nephew Tybalt. Here is the prince of cats, the searcher after mischief, who is drawn to a quarrel as a cat is after fish. This is the courageous captain of compliments, who fights 'as you sing prick-song, keeps time, distance and proportion; rests me his minim, one, two, and the third in your bosom: the very butcher of a silk button . . .' Here is the embodiment of the evil that has besmirched the fair name of Verona; the type of man to whom the taking of life means no more than the killing of a fly and is, in fact, a positive pleasure, since it displays his brilliant dexterity with his rapier. We can imagine as we walk the narrow streets of this ancient city hearing the alarums sounded and the cry of the citizens as a brawl breaks out in the distance. Suddenly in a flash a little cortège races past, led by a dark-haired, pale young man, whose eyes burn with strange excitement; his hand ready on the hilt of his sword—the king of cats has winded his dinner.

The Nurse

To hold our sympathy, but not to stimulate our moral principles, Shakespeare has created one of the most adorable of all his creatures, equal in lovableness to Falstaff, in the Nurse. Here is the nanny of all time, preserved and pickled for our enjoyment and particularly so to-day when such familiars of our infancy are being replaced by certificated specimens trained in the latest wonders of child-psychology and glorying in the title of child-welfare workers. I wonder if Juliet would have been the same exquisite creature, if she had been fed from the thoroughly sterilized bottle of her modern counterpart.

Angelica, however, is the real thing; a peasant woman by origin who, having lost her own child in infancy, was promptly hired and willingly gave her mother's milk to the tender and aristocratic child of the Capulets. So this child became her own;

her own to gossip about and to prattle to. We can well understand how this lonely girl, who finds no help or understanding from her mother, should turn to her Nurse for love and advice. It is to the Nurse that Juliet looks when her mother tells her of the proposed match with Paris—'a man, young lady! Lady, such a man as all the world—why, he's a man of wax'. Again, it is the Nurse who sees the blush that colours her girl's cheeks when the name of the youth with whom she danced is discovered. It is the Nurse who knows of Juliet's meeting with Romeo and who later teases her with Romeo's answer. It is the Nurse who arranges her marriage. All this is right and wins our instant sympathy.

Then comes this Nurse's fall from grace. We must not forget Angelica's humble origin, and her limited capacity for independent action. The match that she has supported against the most strict principles of her employers becomes, at the flash of a sword, a matter of extreme danger to this simple peasant, born with an innate sense of her dependence upon a great family. Romeo kills Tybalt and is publicly disgraced. The Nurse finds herself in danger of discovery, entailing poverty and divorce from all the privileges and perquisites of her position. Her head turns, she does not know what to do or what to think. 'We are undone, lady, we are undone.' She has married her charge to a murderer. But Juliet's steadfastness and determination take the Nurse by storm; she will see her girl through this trouble, though how it will all turn out she cannot say. She sets off to fetch the bridegroom to Juliet's bed. Her nannying instincts are strong and Romeo's distress places him as a child in her arms. It is she and not the Friar who takes the dagger from him, with which he tries to kill himself. She takes it as she would take a dangerous toy from a naughty boy. The risk she is taking in bringing these two lovers together is known to her now, and we can well imagine the anxiety she endures lest they be discovered as they delay their moment of parting and watch the dawn come up. This anxiety is more than her simple mind can stand and, when the master of the household insists on Juliet marrying Paris, her nerve gives way. She can see no outcome to the muddle she has helped to create.

When Juliet turns to her for comfort, she hears these awful words from her Nurse's lips:

'Romeo is banish'd, and all the world to nothing,
That he dare ne'er come back to challenge you;
Or if he do, it needs must be by stealth.
Then, since the case so stands as now it doth,
I think it best you married with the county.'

With these words she and her charge must part company. The Nurse's philosophy and experience will not reach to the rarefied plane of Juliet's love. As if anticipating Juliet's remonstrance, she adds words that will sever the love and trust between child and nanny for ever:

'O, he's a lovely gentleman!
Romeo's a dishclout to him.'

The Rubicon is now crossed—the decisive moment when the child and her nanny must part. To the Nurse there can be no sense in the pursuit of a love that cannot be fulfilled. The danger is too great and even the sin that will ensue from a bigamous second marriage cannot outweigh the danger incurred by disobedience to parents' wishes. The great thing is to keep the matter dark and obey, at no matter what cost. But Juliet has found that other world into which even the best of nannies cannot enter, and she breaks the shackles of one love to enter the shackles of another:

'Go, counsellor,
Thou and my bosom henceforth shall be twain.'

The Nurse can follow no further. She cannot suspect the heights nor the depths of Juliet's passion. She pursues her common task, believing that all is well, and finds her mistress dead. All that is left is lamentation.

The County Paris

About to be allied to the Capulet house, though not yet a member of it, is Paris. We may consider him with the Capulets, for, as heir to their wealth, he must share the view and policies of his future parents-in-law. Paris is often played as a spineless individual, no doubt in order to enhance the manliness of Romeo. I can see no evidence of this in the text, nor do I think it helps the overall interpretation of the play. Romeo's manliness must look after itself, and Paris be permitted to appear in his own colours.

Paris is a nobleman, a count; the constant stressing of this fact by Capulet indicates that the young man's title means a lot to the family. He is by no means deficient in valour. He is referred to as 'the valiant Paris', 'the gallant young and noble gentleman'; he does not hesitate to attack Romeo in the tomb, though the latter begs him to desist. He is good-looking and well-proportioned; in fact, the Nurse considers him 'the properer' man against Romeo's claims. He is rich and of 'fair demesnes', a relative of the Prince himself. In fact, he is a thoroughly suitable suitor and Capulet and his wife have gone to much trouble to arrange the match. We must not think that this marriage, although arranged, is in any way distasteful to Paris. He was the first to broach his suit to Capulet and his conversation to Juliet at Friar Laurence's cell, although stiff and lacking in sensitivity, shows his interest in her; indeed his grief at her death is evidence of his genuine affection. But Paris is no match for the warm-hearted Juliet. There is something of the chill of a highly-bred military cadet about him. He is haughty and correct in bearing. We imagine him to be rather slim and stiff, meticulous about his personal appearance, correct in his courtesies. The Nurse calls him 'a man of wax', thereby likening him, not to something which melts when touched with heat, but to the splendid wax effigies carried in funeral processions. He will be a fitting son-in-law for the Capulets, and his proud nature coupled with his valour will make him a strong upholder of their rights and privileges.

The Capulet Household

Of the other members of the Capulet household we may note the pleasantly garrulous Old Capulet, no doubt a poorer relation who revels in being asked as a guest to the family parties and in recording the exact dates of births, marriages and burials.

Then there are the thoroughly unpleasant retainers, Sampson and Gregory. The former vicious and on the look-out for a quarrel, the latter no less vicious, but more insolent; hiding behind his companion's sword and only ready on the draw when he sees one of his superiors appear in the distance. These are true corner-boys of Elizabethan London, bred by the social conditions of the day and relying on their betters to set them a lamentable example.

Lastly, there is the delightful, if relatively small, part of Peter—a true member of the family of Shakespeare's servants. Illiterate, always cheerful; inquiring of his betters for aid and then hurrying away before the answer is given. We imagine him to be of a mature age, but as simple as a child—a useful and unquestioning escort for the Nurse. He probably occupies a position of some responsibility in Capulet's household, and no doubt chivies the lesser servants around in much the same way as he is chivied by the Nurse. These, then, with the exception of Juliet, are the members of the Capulet household. To Lady Capulet, Tybalt, Paris, Sampson, Gregory and such retainers as are attached to the household we must look for our emphasis on the pride and warlike qualities of the Capulets, for the humour of the play we look to the Nurse, Peter and, in some scenes, to Capulet himself.

The Montagues

The characters of the rival house of Montague are less clearly defined, but Shakespeare seems to prefer this family, or, at all events, he has shown them to us in less warlike and bitter mood. Montague, it is true, is early on the scene of the first brawl, and appears to be laying about him when Capulet arrives, but he obviously regrets the necessity for these feuds in his first few words to Benvolio: 'Who set this ancient quarrel new abroach?' When retribution overtakes the two houses, it is he who offers first to set a seal on the ancient quarrel by raising Juliet's statue in pure gold. He seems to have a sensitive perception of his son's moodiness, and is careful to withdraw and leave Benvolio—his son's contemporary—to find out the cause of it. We must therefore believe him to be a sensible father, but incapable of breaking the evil of civic strife. His wife is, I think, an older woman than Lady Capulet, and is shown to us, in the short glimpses we obtain of her, as a highly sensitive lady. Her attempt to restrain her husband from fighting, her anxiety over her son's moods, and her death caused by grief of Romeo's exile indicate a sensitive and loving wife and mother.

Benvolio

Benvolio is more fully characterized than the head of the household, and as a moral character shows up to great advantage when compared with Tybalt, his opposite number in the Capulet family. As cousins, we presume that he and Romeo have been brought up together. Benvolio appears to have a store of warm-hearted kindliness. It is he who draws from his moody companion the cause of his melancholy. He knows just the right sort of banter to draw Romeo out of his depression. He is a thorough extrovert: interested in other people rather than himself, in which respect he differs totally from his cousin Romeo, and is the best possible companion for him. He is balanced in his judgement: he does his best to avert quarrels and to keep the peace, but being involved he knows how to bear his part. He does not intervene, as Romeo asks him to do, in the fight between Tybalt and Mercutio. I do not think he would consider it right to do so. Romeo has stained his family honour in refusing Tybalt's challenge; Benvolio and Mercutio are obviously shocked and unwilling to let the bully, Tybalt, leave the field unscathed. Mercutio takes up the challenge on Romeo's behalf and Benvolio backs him. But Benvolio's mortification at his friend's lack of courage is short-lived, for a moment later, stung by the news of Mercutio's death, Romeo has taken his revenge and cleared his honour. Benvolio is at once all solicitude for his cousin's safety, and the last we see of him is defending Romeo's conduct to the Prince. Like Horatio in *Hamlet*, we know very little about Benvolio's private life, he does not talk of his own affairs, but we know enough about him from his attitude to others. He is loyal, courageous, warm-hearted and balanced, and his scenes with Mercutio and the Nurse show him to be gay and spirited.

The Montague Household

Once again the preference that Shakespeare shows for the Montagues is visible in the serving men, Abraham and Balthasar. It is the Capulet servants, not the Montagues, who provoke the quarrel, though Abraham will allow no man to better his master, nor will he brook any insults from Sampson. As for Balthasar, he is Romeo's personal servant and from his speech and gentle ways we may presume him to come from an upper-class background; he is a page rather than a serving man. Balthasar is trusted by Romeo with the delicate and secret task of acting as his agent between Mantua and Verona after his exile; he is probably the man who is sent with the rope-ladder to meet the Nurse 'behind the Abbey wall', in which case he is considered by his master to be as 'true as steel'. His sensitive way of telling Romeo of Juliet's death, his plea to his master to show patience, his fears of Romeo's intentions in the tomb all indicate that he knows Romeo's nature and rightly assesses the danger. From glancing at these members of the Montague family and retinue, we may see that they are more gentle, but perhaps less interesting, than their proud and cruel rivals.

The Friar

Closely involved in the innermost secrets of both houses is their mutual confessor, Friar Laurence. We can well imagine what pain it must have given this gentle and well-meaning priest to hear the sins of bitterness, jealousy and even of bloodshed which these proud men and women pour forth in the confessional. Friar Laurence is not a hermit, as has sometimes been supposed, but a member of a Franciscan monastery, who, besides his duties as private confessor to the two great families of the city—an important and influential post—humbles himself in true Franciscan fashion by acting as apothecary to his order. We meet him first at dawn pursuing this common task, collecting weeds and flowers and rejoicing in the grace that a Divine Being has granted to these humble properties.

His simple moral views are seen in this gracious speech,

'For nought so vile that on the earth doth live,
But to the earth some special good doth give . . .'

in which he compares the good and evil that exist in man to
the poisonous and medicinal properties that lie in the 'infant
rind of this small flower'. Friar Laurence has observed the good
and evil that exist side by side in the families he serves. He
has sorrowed over their hatred and pride; he has, perhaps,
prayed for a chance to play some active part in their reconciliation. This chance is granted him, but not in the way he
hoped; for, instead of the Divine Grace being made manifest in
the person of the humble Friar, this well-meaning, Christian
priest is the cause, albeit an unwitting one, of the death of his
two most cherished children. Early on this summer morning
as he gathers his simples he is confronted with what seems to
be the answer to his prayers: Romeo, the son and heir of the
Montagues, desires to marry Juliet, the daughter and heir of
the Capulets. We can imagine the excitement rising within
him. He gently mocks his young charge over his inconstancy
to Rosaline, for he is bubbling over with an inward happiness;
the Grace that he has prayed for is to be granted.

'For this alliance may so happy prove
To turn your household's rancour to pure love.'

Friar Laurence, like all who have to deal with human frailties,
is a cautious man. Although this alliance looks so hopeful for
the future, he counsels moderation of Romeo's passion:

'These violent delights have violent ends
And in their triumph die . . .
Therefore love moderately: long love doth so;
Too swift arrives as tardy as too slow.'

But the love of Romeo and Juliet is no moderate passion. It
has been born in the furnace of hatred that divides brother
from brother, the very heat of which requires a greater heat

to overcome its evil power, lest it shrivel and scorch all that stands near it. Friar Laurence's gentle admonitions are no water to quench the passion of these two lovers and he is swept along in the path of their attachment. His failure to save them from their death-marked love is due, firstly, to his lack of firmness in enforcing a more cautious and moderate approach; secondly, to his lack of worldly wisdom. He has not thought over the implications of this marriage which he solemnizes with such secret joy. The young people are too deeply in love to think for themselves; they have placed their destinies in his hands, but how does he imagine he is going to resolve this trust and gain the consent of their parents? He is no scheming cleric, nor priestly politician; his plans are no more than pious hopes that all will come right in the end.

All too soon these hopes are dashed by the fight between Tybalt and Romeo, and the exile of the latter. His attempt to apply philosophy to Romeo's agony, on hearing of the Prince's sentence, shows how sadly unreal is his knowledge of a passion of such intensity. It is only after the physical struggle with the dagger that Romeo is calmed, and only when the spiritual confessor suggests the far more practical course of ascending Juliet's chamber, that Romeo is restored to sanity. This serious crisis which upsets the hopes of the Friar has, however, a salutary effect on him. From now on he becomes more practical and cunning. He is motivated as always by Christian principles, but he has recourse to a bold ruse when he is forced to grapple with the problem of how to save Juliet from a second marriage. It is no fault of his that the plan goes awry, and his letter to Romeo, entrusted to a brother monk, never reaches its destination. Once he realizes the failure of this scheme he hurries full of foreboding to the tomb alone. It is a desperate race against time; he is too late, Romeo is already dead. It is a case of saving Juliet from herself. The Friar has now learned how helpless he is against the force and majesty of these children's passion for each other. His own life is endangered by the approach of the Watch. He will be arraigned and condemned for unpriestly behaviour; Juliet will never obey him; his cause is lost. But, as he stands a prisoner before the bodies of his beloved children, at the lowest ebb of his fortune, his hopes dashed to the ground, feeling no doubt that God has deserted him, he sees a new light break—Capulet and Montague are holding hands over their children's bodies. Grace has been granted, his prayers have been heard, and he wonders afresh at the mystery of God's ways. A gentle, humble man of God who sought earnestly to cleanse the evil of his fellowmen, but whose knowledge of human passion and whose foresight were insufficient to deal with a situation of such magnitude.

The Prince

Let us now turn to the two great neutral persons, who become involved in this tale of civic strife—the Prince and his kinsman, Mercutio. The Prince seems to have a foot in either camp; for whereas one of his kinsmen, Paris, is to marry into the Capulets, another, Mercutio, is allied by ties of friendship to the young men of the Montague family, but this may be purely fortuitous and we have no reason to suppose that the Prince has any pre-arranged plan of reconciling his warring subjects. We imagine the ruler of Verona to be a comparatively young man, anxious to stamp out the evil that exists in his city-state. We imagine him turning himself and his watchmen into an emergency squad of police. (No doubt the Lord Mayor of London had done the same within Shakespeare's memory.) Armed and ready for the first sign of trouble and having the citizens on his side, he has arranged a system of alarms to give immediate warning of a brawl. We must realize, however, that the situation is delicate; for, in this small city-state—as indeed in the City of London itself, these warring noblemen with their private retinues and their considerable wealth were persons of consequence. Although Escalus is prepared to stop brawls by force, to reprimand the parties and bind them over to keep the peace, he seems unwilling to shoulder the responsibility for stronger action, and only strong action will serve the case. Thus one street fight leads to another, until the Prince is stung into positive action by the murder of two eminent noblemen, his kinsman Mercutio and the powerful supporter of the Capulets—Tybalt.

The Capulets call on him to avenge Tybalt's death. The Montagues plead with him to recognize the justice of Romeo's action. But the Prince has had enough, the time has come to make an example:

> 'Mercy but murders, pardoning those that kill.'

He takes the bit between his teeth and, at the risk of alienating the powerful Montagues, he banishes their son and heir. The next time we see this ruler roused up, it is to hear a different tale. At last the opportunity comes to end the flow of evil by reconciling the enemies:

> 'Where be these enemies? Capulet! Montague!
> See, what a scourge is laid upon your hate
> That heaven finds means to kill your joys with love:
> And I, for winking at your discords too
> Have lost a brace of kinsmen: all are punished.'

To Escalus, Prince of Verona, we are giving the first speech of the Chorus (the second Chorus speech we will cut), for the Chorus's exposition of the plot is the story of the city and of this Prince's reign. The tale of woe which is unfolded in the tomb must weigh heavily on the conscience of the man who is responsible for the maintenance of government and orderly behaviour. What he, through weakness, had failed to achieve was accomplished for him by the untimely death of these two young people. It is an unhappy ghost of the city-state who comes forward to request our patient attention to this play.

Mercutio

Mercutio, 'The Prince's near ally', is the adventurer-poet, a type that Shakespeare clearly much admired. Loose of tongue, of free and happy disposition, always ready with a jest, a good mimic of other people's extravagance—whether it be the coy airs and ruffled dignity of the Nurse, the 'fishified', love-lorn Romeo, the quarrelsome ways of the young bloods, or the lisping affected manners of Tybalt—no extravagance escapes the lash of his tongue. Mercutio is full-blooded: he will fight, he will drink, he will enter into the fun of a masked ball, he will swear, he will talk bawdy and strangest of all, he will talk poetry. To London town of Shakespeare's day came many strange characters: merchants from outlandish countries, sailors with tales of wonder and adventure, and soldiers who had served with Sidney and Essex with their rough camp talk and their coarse jests. Shakespeare mixed with all these, learning much from them, translating many of them into his plays. Who inspired Mercutio we shall probably never know, but from one, or perhaps several, he observed that an adventurous life does not only breed coarse talk and rough ways, but that often it can be allied to a strange fantasy of imagination, bred perhaps round the watch-fires on the eve of battle, when the world takes on a strange unreality, and the imagination takes wing to the familiar scenes and secret places of boyhood—to the great forest near Stratford, to the old tales of the country folk about the strange faery people who lived there and to those dreams:

> 'Which are the children of an idle brain,
> Begot of nothing but vain fantasy,
> Which is as thin of substance as the air,
> And more inconstant than the wind, who woos
> Even now the frozen bosom of the north,
> And, being anger'd, puffs away in haste,
> Turning his face to the dew-dropping south.'

It is night in Verona and the masked companions have paused on their way to the dance. There is an indolent feeling; Romeo is melancholy; the air is heavy; the torches cast a strange light on the weird masks of the party, and Mercutio's fantasy is born. How different when we see him next; for this quicksilver creature will jump from the highest poetry to the lowest bawdy talk in a flash. Mercutio, despite his mockery and banter, has a genuine affection for Romeo and Benvolio who are his juniors in age and experience, but though he despises the evil nature of Tybalt, he does not take the part of the Montagues in their brawls. It is true dramatic irony that causes him to take up the insult offered to their son and to die defending the

Montagues' honour, stabbed under the arm of Romeo himself.
Even in death he has an oath and a jest on his lips:

> 'A plague o' both your houses!'
> 'No, 'tis not so deep as a well, nor so wide as a church
>   door,
> But 'tis enough, 'twill serve: ask for me to-morrow, and
>   you shall find me a grave man.'

But the worst of all ironies for Mercutio is to be killed by
Tybalt; 'a braggart, a rogue, a villain, that fights by the book
of arithmetic.' Mercutio mocked the world, though his heart
was true to his friends, he even mocked at death and Benvolio
says of him:

> 'That gallant spirit hath aspir'd the clouds,
> Which too untimely scorn'd the lowly earth.'

The Lovers

Lastly we come to the lovers whose names this play bears—
Romeo and Juliet.

We note at once that, whereas the other characters in the
play, largely because of their greater maturity, remain static,
Romeo and Juliet grow from youth to early manhood and
womanhood during the action of the play. Romeo's age is
uncertain, but he begins the play in the throes of the sort of
adolescent love-affair which we associate with the late teen-age
period. His love for Rosaline is, of course, unrequited; being
a friend of the Capulets she has probably good reason to treat
his advances with coldness. Consequently his love is thrown
in upon itself and this, coupled with an emotional and introspective nature, is likely, as his father fears, to have dangerous
effects upon his health and outlook. Romeo shows all the signs
typical of the state known as love-lorn youth: walking alone
in the early morning, choosing shady and melancholy ways,
shutting himself up in his room and refusing to join with his
companions. This state is not incurable as Benvolio and
Mercutio know. The sad-faced young man can be made to
smile and, being possessed of a quick and ready tongue, can

be roused to a battle of wits with Mercutio and win his spurs.
He is dragged seemingly unwillingly to the Capulets' dance,
though secretly he probably enjoys the fuss that is being made
of him, and once he reaches it the whole world is turned
upside down. Romeo would never have believed he could
meet one fairer than his love, but a glance at the girl who
enriches the hand of Paris and the torches themselves seem dim.
Rosaline is forgotten, never to be mentioned again:

'Did my heart love till now? Forswear it, sight!
For I ne'er saw true beauty till this night.'

The shy and beautiful meeting of the lovers in a stiff and
measured dance by themselves is properly becoming to such
a fancy-dress occasion, and is a gem of brilliant writing.

This meeting is the first milestone in Romeo's progress to
maturity. Gone is the introspective moon-struck boy. Here is
the young, active lover climbing the wall of his love's garden,
oblivious of the taunts and jests of his companions and of the
danger he is running. Romeo is no longer in love with love,
he is in love with Juliet. He is bold in his protestations, pressing in
his suit and is rewarded with the exchange of his vow for hers.
Now all his moodiness is thrown to the wind; there is not a
minute to be lost; he is off post-haste to Friar Laurence to
arrange a secret marriage. His words tumble over each other
as he tells his wondrous tale. When he next meets his friends,
they find him much changed. He repays jest with jest and pun
with pun, till Mercutio complains that his wits begin to fail.
This is a new Romeo; no longer the boy 'without his roe, like
a dried herring' whom Mercutio teased, but a young man in
love with a real girl, who feels himself on top of the world.
His mind is moving swiftly; there is a marriage to be arranged;
a new life is opening out in which there is someone else to
think of other than himself. The introvert has changed his
skin; he has discovered the world that lies outside his narrow
horizon. But Romeo's horizons are still not wide enough. He
can see no further than the immediate future. How is this rash
and sudden marriage to be implemented? He has not thought,
he cannot look thus far into the future:

'Do thou but close our hands with holy words'

he says to the Friar,

'Then love-devouring death do what he dare,
It is enough I may but call her mine.'

It is true that forebodings cross his mind:

'I am afear'd
Being in night, all this is but a dream,
Too flattering sweet to be substantial.'

Warnings are given him, too, by the Friar:

'These violent delights have violent ends.'

But Romeo is young and passionate. He will adventure for 'such merchandise'. He has yet to learn the value of calm thought and proper preparation. This is to be the second phase of Romeo's progress to manhood. It is brought home to him by a rude shock, no less than the death of his friend, Mercutio; killed under his arm because of his own unwillingness to accept Tybalt's challenge. There follows remorse and a realization of the cruel facts of his position:

'Ah sweet Juliet,
Thy beauty makes me thus effeminate,
And in my temper softens valour's steel!'

He had indeed forgotten who he is and in what circumstances he is placed. Once he realizes his responsibilities, the passionate lover becomes the no less passionate champion of his family and the avenger of his friend. And so to his exile, and his passionate agony—the agony of a man who has been living, oblivious of the unpleasant facts of life, and who now faces the terrible muddle into which his passion has plunged both himself and his newly married wife. He hadn't thought; his youthful, Italian blood had prevented him from considering what was really best for him and Juliet. But, then, we can scarcely blame either of them; they are young and very much in love, and, as we stated earlier, older and wiser heads had failed to restrain them. Moreover, we must not overlook the climate and surroundings of their passion. It was not born in a quiet country lane, nor in the back seat of a cinema, nor on an ocean voyage; it was bred in the dunghill of hatred, in the teeth of cruel opposition. As we have said already and emphasize again, a love that is born under such conditions is not likely to be gentle and moderate. It was not the fault of these children that their love was too intense for this world; the blame lies with the two households whose jealousy and mistaken sense of honour allowed no other sort of love to blossom.

Romeo's passionate agony is followed by his tender farewell to his wife. Awakened from their brief moment of earthly happiness, they stand together in the first light of dawn and face the ordeal of parting. Romeo is thinking now only of his young wife, trying desperately to allay her fears, to hold out hopes for their future which seems so black and hopeless. He pursues his course to Mantua, is filled with hope that things will come right, when he hears the awful news—Juliet is dead. For the second time in his young life, the world is turned upside down, but this time his passion, although more deeply felt, is contained. One single outburst:

'Is it e'en so? Then I defy you stars'

and then comes his last stage of growth. A calm, though terrible, intention takes hold of him. He knows his purpose; life has ceased to hold out any future for him; he must follow Juliet to the tomb. He is cunning and cool in his preparations, exact and methodical in his thought. He remembers the Apothecary most likely to serve his purpose; he pays him adequately; he writes to his father; he gives strict and careful instructions to his page; he tries to avoid trouble with Paris, but nothing, not even Paris's life, must stand in his way. His mind is made up, he is resolute. This is no longer the emotional, hot-blooded youth of the second phase, but the calm and decided man, who, however terrible his purpose, is no longer swayed by emotion or passion. He goes to his death with his eyes open both to the future and to the past.

Romeo has lived and suffered, though young in years, he is

old in experience when his 'sea-sick weary bark' is 'dashed on the rocks'. Thus we see the growth of his character through three separate stages: the introvert, love-lorn boy, the hot-blooded, passionate youth and the developed, calm man setting out on his journey into the unknown. Three major events in his life are responsible for these changes: his meeting with Juliet, the death of Mercutio, and the news of Juliet's death.

Juliet likewise undergoes her metamorphoses. At first we see the child of fourteen, playful with her Nurse, obedient and awe-struck by her mother. But already at this stage we notice that this girl has a mind of her own. For all her innocence and childishness she will not accept blindly that her life shall be ruled by others. When her mother requests her to consider the suit of the rich and important young suitor, her reply is guarded:

> 'I'll look to like, if looking liking move:
> But no more deep will I endart mine eye
> Than your consent gives strength to make it fly.'

Juliet's determination is a source of some irritation to her tyrannical old father, who likes immediate compliance with his orders:

> 'A peevish self-will'd harlotry it is . . . .'
> 'Hang thee, young baggage! Disobedient wretch . . . .'
> 'How now my head-strong! Where have you been gadding?'

And even allowing for Capulet's tetchiness, we must admit that Juliet is a determined young lady. She is also possessed of a marked sense of foreboding, we might call it second-sight. To some extent she shares this with Romeo, who is also prone to premonitions of disaster. She has scarcely met Romeo when she feels the first premonition:

> 'My only love sprung from my only hate,
> Too early seen unknown, and known too late.'

And in the moment of ecstasy when Romeo comes to her

140

balcony window, she again feels a warning hand placed on her shoulder:

'I have no joy in this compact to-night:
It is too rash, too unadvis'd, too sudden,
Too like the lightning, which doth cease to be
Ere one can say "It lightens".'

These warnings, which come like flashes upon her inner-mind, culminate in her farewell to her husband, when she imagines she sees him dead and lying in his tomb; and in her lonely agony as she prepares to take the potion she vividly pictures the grisly accoutrements of the tomb in which she is to be immured.

This child, then, has need of all the strength and determination that lie within her to go forward in her love for Romeo against such forebodings of disaster and against the full opposition of her parents. We must not forget what her defiance of her parents means in the circumstances; it is an act of treason against her family's honour. But Juliet's love has all the ardent affection, all the passion of giving that lie in a young girl's power. The child has turned into the young lady in love. The chrysalis has burst open and the butterfly has emerged. Neither visions of disaster, nor parents' rage, nor family honour can outweigh her love. She lives now only for Romeo. Time becomes her enemy. She waits for what seems an unbearable time for her Nurse's return with news of him. She flies to him unashamed, heedless of maidenly modesty, intent only on this power which is stronger than herself. She waits again begging the fiery-footed steeds to gallop apace and hasten the night that will bring the consummation of her love, but this time her Nurse brings no teasing tale; a story is blurted out, blurred in its outlines—a story of death. Juliet jumps to the awful conclusion that Romeo is killed, only to hear that this is not so, but that Romeo has killed Tybalt. Her head is swimming, her brain reels, she cannot think clearly. Romeo has failed her, has deceived her, has ruined their happiness. Then loyalty comes rushing over her with the Nurse's exclamation,

'Shame come to Romeo'. The child-wife rises to her husband's defence:

'Blister'd be thy tongue
For such a wish! He was not born to shame.
Upon his brow shame is ashamed to sit.'

She struggles with her whirling mind to find what this disaster will mean for the future—Romeo is banished, their happiness is at an end. Exhausted, like a child, she asks for her mother and her father. But there can come no comfort from them; she is Romeo's wife, and they are weeping over the man he killed. She must go on alone—she has become a woman. Romeo comes to her and the morning light brings the fearful moment of their parting. At first she will not let him go, and then the woman, mindful of his danger, urges him away. Now she is utterly alone to face a yet harder and crueller problem— she is ordered to marry Paris. Juliet, the wife of Romeo, will not consent to this sin, no matter what threats are heaped upon her, no matter whether her Nurse and her mother turn from her. But she has need of cunning to maintain her independence; wilfulness and disobedience can be worn down by heartless and determined parents, so Juliet must act and think boldly. She seeks the Friar's aid and, terrible as her task is, difficult and dangerous as her role must be, she goes through it with womanly courage. Consider the risks she takes she must seemingly consent to marry Paris, deceive her parents, sort her attire for the wedding, arrange to sleep alone. If the effects of the potion fail to take effect, she will have to kill herself or be married to Paris, and she lays the dagger ready for this awful eventuality; if the effects work off before the time appointed for her rescue she will awake locked in the family vault, lying side by side with corpses. It is no slight undertaking for a girl of fourteen. To undertake so great a risk requires a coolness, a boldness and a cunning unknown to the child who ran out to hear her mother's instructions before the masked ball. Juliet, like Romeo, has grown up. There remains the awakening in the tomb, when joy enters her heart in the belief that the plan has succeeded, and then a terrible irony follows. Her husband has arrived before she awoke and has killed himself believing her to be dead. Like Romeo, when he hears of her supposed death, Juliet receives this most terrible blow of all with outward calm. Hitherto she has struggled against her misfortunes, has turned to her Nurse, to the Friar, to her mother or to God for help, but now there is not a word of grief, not a call for help, only her firm order to the Friar:

'Go, get thee hence for I will not away.'

Like Romeo, she knows her destiny; as a wife and a woman she goes to meet her husband. The part of Juliet, then, like the part of Romeo, is a progressive part. The actress has to understand this delicate period of progress from childhood to womanhood, and to endue that progress with the strength of character, sweetness of disposition, ardour of passion and absolute understanding of giving herself to her lover. To do this properly she must be neither a purely innocent child in whose presence we feel embarrassment, nor yet a mature woman in whose fresh innocence we cannot believe. Juliet must hang half-way between girlhood and womanhood, capable of making us believe in the former state no less than in her power of understanding the latter. The forcing of either will destroy the magic of this character, for the character of Juliet cannot be acted, it must be lived.

The destruction of these two harmless and innocent beings was inevitable from their first meeting:

'The fearful passage of their death-marked love,
And the continuance of their parents' rage,
Which, but their children's end, nought could remove
. . .'

This death-marked love was too like the lightning to remain fixed on earth. The circumstances under which it was born made it impossible for it to last. The deaths of Romeo and Juliet set them free to join the stars, which looked down upon the orchard where they plighted their troth. But by their deaths they achieved what neither the power of the State, nor the teachings of the Church could accomplish, the reconcilement of their two houses. Their end, then, was no useless sacrifice, their tomb no grave, but 'a feasting presence full of light'—a light that taught both Prince and Friar, nobleman and citizen, how they had erred from the path of charity and social responsibility. Round the golden statues of the Montague and Capulet children the dreaded alarums were silenced, the brawls were stilled, the hands of the parents were joined, as the city-state of Verona bowed its head in sorrow and shame:

'Go hence, to have more talk of these sad things;
Some shall be pardoned and some punished;
For never was a story of more woe
Than this of Juliet and her Romeo.'

POSTSCRIPT

The success of this production of *Romeo and Juliet* seemed like one of those improbable endings with which Moliére, and sometimes Shakespeare, conclude their comedies.

After only two seasons in its new home, the Old Vic had fallen upon troubled times; internal dissension, bad luck and bad judgement had lowered the prestige of the theatre, and there were not a few who had prepared its funeral oration. In August, 1953, we were faced with a new season which could only be carried through if unusual success was achieved in the first few months. Though failure and criticism often prove a spur to the artist, anxiety and lack of confidence are not the best background for creation. The stage artist, be he player, designer or producer, is abnormally sensitive to failure and his job lays him more open than most to criticism. He needs to be hedged round with confidence; to feel that, however much the outside world may doubt him, he has the trust of all who work with him. Doubts and mistrust in his abilities, which might spur less vulnerable persons to success, are liable to produce a break-down of self-confidence, which can spread like a bush-fire through the theatre. If the actor loses his belief in himself, his own performance will suffer; if the producer loses his belief in himself, all the performances will suffer. Realizing this, the Directors and management of the Old Vic generously and wisely gave me their confidence, and left me alone to carry through my task.

This task seemed harder in that the play had to be staged twice; once on the open stage of the Edinburgh Assembly Hall, and again at the Old Vic. In effect this proved more of a help than a hindrance, for the open stage gave the play a vigour and pace that might well have been missed had it been prepared only for the conventional stage of the theatre.

Controversy rages over the value of the open stage for Shakespeare. Protagonists of the picture-frame complain of their inability to concentrate on the actor's face, which results from his acting to an audience on three sides of him; they regret the loss of illusion resulting from the limitation of stage machinery and the proximity of the actor to the audience. The open stage champions retort that by sweeping away the tinsel of the theatre, the play is brought closer to the author's intention; that by bringing the actor out to meet the audience, we establish the contact that existed in the Elizabethan playhouse; that by removing the necessity for scenery, the production regains the placelessness of its original.

There is truth on both sides of the argument. So far as *Romeo* was concerned, the crowd scenes, the fights, the dance in Capulet's house, the scenes in the streets and outside Laurence's cell gained immeasurably from the open stage. The balcony scene, the tomb scene and Juliet's potion scene were more effective at the Vic. From the actor's point of view there is a new excitement and stimulus to be gained from the open stage and it was interesting to find that the older players, who might be expected to be less enthusiastic at the idea of losing their familiar surroundings, left Edinburgh as confirmed 'open stagers'.

The stimulation of meeting the challenge of this open stage, the sense of team work which it brought to our efforts to solve the problems which it presented, and the excitement of feeling the participation of the audience all round us gave us the confidence to bring about the success that seemed so improbable, and placed the Old Vic Theatre firmly on the road to the future.

THE MERCHANT OF VENICE

THE MERCHANT OF VENICE
Old Vic Theatre
6th January 1953

ANTONIO		DOUGLAS CAMPBELL
SALERIO	Friends to Antonio and	TONY VAN BRIDGE
SALANIO	Bassanio	PATRICK WYMARK
BASSANIO		ROBERT URQUHART
GRATIANO		WILLIAM SQUIRE
LORENZO		RICHARD GALE
NERISSA		JANE WENHAM
PORTIA		IRENE WORTH
STEPHANO	Servants to Portia	JAMES MAXWELL
BALTHASAR		ERIC THOMPSON
SHYLOCK		PAUL ROGERS
THE PRINCE OF MOROCCO		GEORGE MURCELL
LAUNCELOT GOBBO		KENNETH CONNOR
OLD GOBBO		NEWTON BLICK
LEONARDO, Servant to Bassanio		JOHN BRESLIN
JESSICA		CLAIRE BLOOM
THE PRINCE OF ARRAGON		JOHN WARNER
TUBAL, A JEW		WOLFE MORRIS
THE DUKE OF VENICE		DANIEL THORNDIKE

LADIES, ATTENDANTS, VENETIANS, MASQUERS AND OFFICERS
OF THE COURT:
BARBARA GRIMES, PHYLLIDA LAW, JOAN PLOWRIGHT,
JOHN BRESLIN, ALAN DOBIE, BERNARD KILBY, DOUGLAS
RAIN, DENIS RAYMOND, LLOYD RECKORD, BRUCE SHAR-
MAN, ERIC THOMPSON.

Sets and Costumes by Roger Furse.
Music composed by Christopher Whelan.

The heartbreak and the loneliness . . . the evil and the cunning

SHYLOCK: Paul Rogers

[Photograph: Angus McBean, London]

'Descend, for you must be my torchbearer'

[Photograph: Angus McBean, London]

'Lock up my doors'

SHYLOCK: Paul Rogers   JESSICA: Claire Bloom

THE MERCHANT OF VENICE

G RANVILLE BARKER called *The Merchant of Venice* a fairy tale. It is in fact two fairy tales; the tale of the Princess destined to be won by the lover who solves the riddle of the caskets, and the tale of the wicked Oriental money-lender who tries to encompass the death of the honest merchant. These two stories are eventually amalgamated by an exciting, if rather improbable, trial scene in which the Princess and her maid disguise themselves as men, and the whole rounded off with a lyrical ending, in which the merchant is rescued and the lovers united. Like all fairy stories *The Merchant of Venice* contains much that, if looked at too closely, seems improbable; such as the business of the caskets and the disguise of Portia and Nerissa as a lawyer and his clerk. Indeed, critics, scornful of its ingenuosity, have marvelled at its popularity. Some of these critics find Portia priggish and pedantic, others accuse Bassanio of being a calculating fortune-hunter, others maintain that the jingoism and intolerance of the Christians destroy the play's equilibrium, turning it from a comedy into an intolerble melodrama of Jew-baiting.

The truth lies in the fact that the play is a fairy tale, and in the acting of it we must hold fast to the principles upon which fairy tales are founded. These principles have little to do with material probabilities, with psychological complexes, or with introvert personalities, which are the stock-in-trade of naturalistic playwrights.

A fairy tale demands firstly, the telling of a plain, unvarnished tale and secondly, the simple, epic type of characterization which divides the world between the good and the bad without any attempt to linger over probability or motivation. To tell a plain, unvarnished tale upon the stage we need speed, clarity and dramatic tension. We must not try to embellish the action by extraneous effects nor ponder too much over the thought-process of the personalities. What matters is the story and the atmosphere of the play, not the subtleties of characterization and behaviour. The apparent difficulty of accepting the naïve simplicity of this story has led some producers and players to find new meanings behind the motivation of the characters; to suggest that Antonio is degenerate or that Bassanio is only out to win a fortune, to twist the sympathy of the play on to Shylock, to show Jessica and Lorenzo as a couple of unscrupulous thieves or to vilify Gratiano and the Venetians. Such attempts to impose psychological motivation on the characters and to create dramatic situations which the play does not possess make nonsense of the love story, destroy the poetry and render the last scene—perhaps one of the most lyrical in the English language—a mockery of itself.

Location and Costume

I do not propose that we should load this production with realistic scenery. Our task is to give the play the lightness and magic of a fairy tale and not to move ponderously round the ghetto of Venice and the cypress groves of Belmont. Nor do I think we should clothe it in some vague quatro-cento convention about which Shakespeare knew nothing at all. A modern audience has a certain idea of Venice derived principally from the painters Canaletto and Guardi, and the simplest way to indicate Venice to an audience is to follow in the spirit of these two masters, but without deliberate imitation. Critics will no doubt pride themselves on their historical knowledge by pointing out that the play is costumed at least a hundred years later than the Elizabethan age. What a time they would have had at the Globe with the players of Macbeth, and Antony and Cleopatra in ruffs and farthingales, or with Garrick as Lear in baroque finery! Our object will be to establish Venice by the quickest and most easily acceptable means. The principal scene will be a piazza in Venice, presented in the manner of the perspective paintings of the Venetian school without realistic details or embroideries. The problem of alternating Venice and Belmont is considerable, for since we no longer possess the bare platform of the Globe, we are forced to give some kind of visual illusion to our scenery, and visual illusion to these two alternating locations means scene-change and the evil of stage waits.

My object is, as I have said, to endow the play with the magic of the fairy story and Belmont of all places must possess a magic quality. It will therefore be represented by a little white pavilion—the pavilion of the caskets—which will rise up from the floor of the stage on a lift. By this means, and without further alterations of scenery, one scene will follow on the other without interruption and we shall not disturb the flow of the play by chopping it up with ponderous scene changes. This continuous flow of scene into scene is the essential unity of action which is no less a rule of Shakespeare's theatre, than are the famous unities of time and place postulated by Boileau for the seventeenth-century neo-classical theatre. This simple device will be our setting, and all we need beyond it will be a vague stone background for the court scene.

The Problem of Shylock

But there is a major problem in the handling of this fairy tale which cannot be easily overcome—it is Shylock. Shakespeare was a playwright first and a story-teller second. As a playwright he gave birth to people rather than to stories, and once you start giving birth to people you cannot control the result. Milton wrote *Paradise Lost* with the pious intention of glorifying God and the good angels and vilifying Satan and the rebel angels, but the most vital character in *Paradise Lost* is Satan. From the time of the earliest mystery plays the audience's interest was aroused more by the devils issuing from the fiery mouth of hell, than by the saintly creatures walking in the gardens of paradise; and Judas on the stage is not without our sympathy. For this reason, consciously or unconsciously,

Shakespeare has kept the Portia story separate from the Shylock story, and Belmont from Venice. The two stories are only brought together when the opportunity arises for a scene in which Portia can meet and defeat the Jew.

Shakespeare took his character of Shylock from an Italian Renaissance source, a source which painted this figure of the Jew in the blackest possible colours. As an Englishman of his epoch he accepted the evilness of the Jew and he set out to please the groundlings by baiting him. The choice of subject was apt enough, for in 1594 public sentiment in London had been roused by one of those traditional outbreaks of anti-Zionism which recur throughout history. Shylock was conceived as a villain, and, in the simple tradition of the fairy story, he is recognizable as such from his first entrance. 'Three thousand ducats; well . . .' 'For three months; well . . .' 'Antonio shall become bound; well . . .' This repetition of the word 'well' has the same effect as the 'Ha! Ha!' of the pantomime demon-king. The tradition of pantomime demands that the demon-king should make his first entrance on the left side of the stage, whereas the fairy-queen enters on the right. Once the villain has exposed his evil intention—be it to kill Aladdin or to ruin Cinderella—the fairy-queen must change her wand from her right hand to her left so as to protect her heart from evil and place herself in a position to protect her protégées. But in the process of creating this demon-king, at the moment when inspiration took over from the simple act of story-telling, Shylock inconveniently started writing Shakespeare, instead of Shakespeare writing Shylock.

This Jew whom Shakespeare recognized as the typical bugbear of his age became a human being instead of a monster. The character grew in roundness and in dignity; his wicked imprecations against Christians became the haunted, homeless call of the outcast. Indeed he might have crossed over the stage and the fairy-queen with her wand might have been forced to retire, had not Shakespeare kept the two stories separate. No doubt the actors of the Globe, in search of a popular theme, confided to their resident dramatist the task of writing a play about the universally unpopular Jew, but they overlooked the fact that they were giving this task to a man who created characters as a mother creates a child, and that once the act of generation had begun the results were not always as predictable as the device employed by Jacob for producing parti-coloured lambs.

Shakespeare, like Milton, fashioned his villain without being fully conscious of what sort of animal he was creating, and Shylock, like Satan, refused to be restricted by the conventions of popular belief and prejudice. Even if Shakespeare and Milton shared with their contemporaries certain articles of belief and certain prejudices of their times—beliefs and prejudices which they would naturally express in their outer lives; in their inner lives, by virtue of which they were artists, they tuned-in to the inner truth about Satan and Shylock and caught the pity, the pride, the heartbreak and the loneliness which lie behind the bitterness, the evil and the cunning of the popular villain.

Thus Shylock enters *The Merchant of Venice* as a creation of Shakespeare, the Renaissance Englishman, and leaves it as the creation of Shakespeare, the artist. Our task is to reconcile the simple fairy story of *The Merchant of Venice*, in which probability and psychological truth are discarded in favour of 'magic casements opening on a sea of fairy-lands forlorn', with this realistic figure of the outcast of the ages, so close to our own experience and so demanding of our sympathy.

Without this reconciliation we cannot hope to preserve the equilibrium of the play and the fairy story will turn into callous Jew-baiting. Our task will be to observe a strict balance of the black and white elements of the characterization without denying the Jew his humanity. This can be done if we preserve the fairy story and do not try to embellish it with realism. The lovers must be kept simple and likeable and the villain must not be allowed to step out of the frame and knock pitifully at Jessica's door, nor pass like a shadow across the moon-lit lawns of Belmont, as has been done in some productions. Let us, therefore, be content with what Shakespeare has written. It is fine enough, and there is no need to embellish it by trying to turn it into propaganda for anti- or pro-Zionism.

Now to preserve this balance look first of all at the characters of the lovers and accept them at their simple face value. Bassanio is a gentleman by birth and in a fairy story a gentleman must be a little too liberal of his purse, a little too free in his outlook on life, as well as being loyal to his friends and genuine in his love of his mistress. That is Shakespeare's Bassanio, and the play is jeopardized if we attempt to embellish his character with deeper motives or sinister intents. Portia is rich and in the tradition of fairy stories a lady born in the purple must have a ready wit and prove her worth in the world; she must not win her spurs by a shabby trick played on a lonely, pathetic outcast. Lorenzo and Jessica elope because they are in love, not because Lorenzo is trying to steal Shylock's ducats. Gratiano and Nerissa, being lesser-born copies of Bassanio and Portia, are permitted to be broader in their outlook and behaviour than the principals, but they must remain fundamentally happy, simple people. In the behaviour of all these people we see the familiar pattern of Shakespeare's comedy. I do not mean that these people are merely replicas of similar figures in other comedies, but in Shakespeare's comedy the lovers work to a pattern and that pattern is a love-dance or mating masquerade in which Beatrice and Benedick, Berowne and Rosaline, Helena and Demetrius, Rosalind and Orlando, Katherine and Petruchio, all dance to a measure. The pattern of this dance must be kept. And so the advice I want you to follow is to keep the pattern, dance the measure, tell the story, and to do so simply and clearly. Remember what is required is style acting, not naturalistic acting. Let Shakespeare make the characters; do not try to embellish them with fancies of your own. So much for the white personalities. Now for the black.

Like Malvolio, Shylock is fundamentally a butt for the mockery of these dancing figures. Malvolio and Shylock may nearly cause our tears as well as our mockery, but they must not lose their place in the dance. Shylock will, of course, emerge as a real person; for the heart that beats beneath his Jewish gaberdine is uncompromisingly human and his words, vital and bitter as they may have been when Shakespeare wrote them, are far more so now through circumstances which have nothing whatsoever to do with *The Merchant of Venice*. These modern circumstances, however, and the pity that mixed itself with Shakespeare's ink as he drew the portrait, are no reason for sentimentalizing Shylock. The Jew is neither tragic nor comic, he is the villain, and although we may shed a tear as he walks alone and broken from the court, we must not lose sight of his villainy, nor must the fairy story lose its balance through him.

Antonio's Melancholy

Why is Antonio sad? The problem has been left unresolved by Shakespeare, nor is it necessary to the action to know the psychological cause of it, any more than to know the psychological cause of Leontes's jealousy which opens, equally abruptly, *The Winter's Tale*. This sadness of Antonio has the elements of the beginning of a fairy story—'Once upon a time there was a merchant who was sad.' Although we must accept this situation in the fairy story way, just as we accept the fact that 'old King Cole was a merry old soul', I will here agree that the actor has need of some excuse on which to found his sadness, for though merriness is acceptable without reason, sadness is not. Is Antonio sad because he has a subconscious fore-knowledge of the trouble ahead? It seems most unlikely, since his affairs are going well. We know he is not in love, nor preoccupied with business. We know also that his close friend, Bassanio, has promised to tell him about a secret pilgrimage to a certain lady; that is the only known fact about his immediate mood, happy or sad, at the beginning of the play. The first question he addresses to Bassanio, as soon as the two are left alone, is 'Well, tell me now, what lady is the same to whom you swore a secret pilgrimage'. It is a direct question requiring a direct answer. But why should Antonio be sad that his friend has a love affair on hand? I don't know for certain, nor do I think a certain answer can be found, but I think we can agree without misconstruing the friendship of Antonio and Bassanio that their friendship depends more on emotional attraction than on common interest, for Antonio is a merchant and

Bassanio is a gentleman. The sad, industrious Antonio is attracted by this gay young spendthrift. This does not mean that he is jealous of his friend's love affair, indeed the signs are against such a conclusion, considering that Antonio furnishes Bassanio for the expedition to Belmont at peril of his own life. There is perhaps a clue to this sadness worth consideration. When Bassanio hints to Antonio of a plan he has in mind for improving his fortune, Antonio says:

> 'I pray you, good Bassanio, let me know it;
> And if it stand, as you yourself still do,
> *Within the eye of honour,* be assured,
> My purse, my person, my extremest means,
> Lie all unlock'd to your occasions.'

Antonio is asking if Bassanio's plan to woo Portia is a strictly honourable affair. Portia's wealth is well known; suitors from all parts of the world travel to Belmont to gain possession of her fortunes. Antonio knows that his friend's fortunes are at a low ebb, that he has an easy way with money. Bassanio has just admitted as much to him. Is Bassanio joining up with the other adventurers with the sole object of enriching himself. Is he wooing Portia only for her fabulous fortune which is what later critics have accused him of doing? This is, I think, Antonio's fear and causes his melancholy, for he loves Bassanio and he would like to see him happily married. He would like to befriend him as an older and wiser man, who has no son of his own, and these Elizabethan gallants were attractive, feckless individuals as Shakespeare knew in his early sonnets. Then Bassanio tells this tale:

> 'In Belmont is a lady richly left,
> And she is fair, and fairer than that word,
> Of wondrous virtues; sometimes from her eyes
> I did receive fair speechless messages:
> Her name is Portia . . .'

And with these words, Antonio's sadness leaves him. Bassanio wants to go to Belmont because he has fallen in love; how deeply he probably does not yet know, but the glimpse of Portia that he has already caught in her father's time has remained fresh in his heart as her first glimpse of him has in hers. Antonio accepts the genuineness of Bassanio's passion and is prepared to do everything that lies within his power to help him. Perhaps Shakespeare felt the same melancholy about Mr. W. H.

The Salads

Are they Salerio and Solanio, or Salanio and Salarino, these two gentlemen who accompany Antonio and endeavour to find out the cause of his sadness? Not only are their names indeterminate—the Quarto has one version and the Folio another—but they seem somewhat indeterminate as people, to whom actors have given the derogatory name of the Salads. Traditionally they are played by the youngest and worst actors in the company. I know, because I once played one of them myself and was chosen to do so because as well as being bad I was thought, erroneously, to be a well-to-do actor who wouldn't want a salary. This was, of course, before the days of Equity.

Traditionally, too, and perhaps as a result of the way they are so often cast, these parts are extensively cut. Who are these walking gentlemen who talk so much and appear to provide no more than a necessary cover-up for a scene change? Have they any character and what is their purpose? If we look at what they say we are most likely to hit upon the answer. So first let us close our eyes to the young Salads, with their tights in folds and their wigs askew, and listen to their words. In the first scene, there appears, to me at any rate, to be a difference of character between them; for whereas Salarino, alias Salerio, is garrulous and rather futile, Salanio, alias Solanio, is both sober and restrained. It may be fancy but I cannot accept them as young sparks, nor do I think that Antonio, a wise and royal merchant, would walk round Venice with two young gabbling puppies. I believe them to be merchants like Antonio, though not so prosperous. Perhaps their trade is confined to Venice, whereas we know Antonio is engaged in the import-export business. I find the words they speak to be more consistent with the sort of elderly merchants who stroll round the piazza of Venice or sit upon 'Change, than with young Elizabethan gallants. Moreover, I believe the Venetians in this play belong to two social classes: the merchant class of Antonio, and the gentleman class of Bassanio. If Bassanio has his Gratiano and Lorenzo to represent the companions with whom a gentleman associates, surely Antonio is entitled to a merchant's companions? And I believe this class grouping is important. The sympathy of an Elizabethan audience for Bassanio is enhanced by the fact that he, a gentleman, rushes to the aid of his friend, a merchant. Moreover, when Bassanio and his gentlemen companions go to Belmont and Antonio has been imprisoned by Shylock, we must feel that the merchant has been deserted by these powerful friends, but if Antonio is being followed round in the scene with Shylock and the gaoler (Act III, Sc. 3) by a gaily-dressed young gallant, the effect of his aloneness is lost; so, too, is the effect of the return of Bassanio and Gratiano. The purpose of the Salads is, I believe, to emphasize the position in the play of the merchant of Venice. But it is also more than that; what we said about the use of these two figures to pad out the play is also relevant, though for a different reason than merely to give time for a scene change. Their job is to build up the situations and prepare us for the action that is to follow. In Act II, Sc. 8 they inform us of the successful elopement of Jessica and Lorenzo; in this and in Act III, Sc. 1, they prepare us for Antonio's disaster, and build up Shylock's rage at the loss of his daughter and his ducats in such a way as to make us laugh at Shylock. Perhaps Shakespeare knew the danger of Shylock winning our sympathy by the discovery of Jessica's flight if he were allowed to play the scene of his return from the banquet on the stage. Henry Irving spotted the plum that Shakespeare had deliberately avoided, and like the great old actor he was, played the scene that was not written and cut the scene that was. So these despised Salads act as a chorus to the play as well as emphasizing and strengthening the merchant class against the Jews; and what is more right in *The Merchant of Venice* than to have merchants as a chorus.

Portia

Now let us take ship to Belmont and to the story of the caskets—a story which has often been declared intolerably boring. The mistress of this magic island is young, she says so; she is rich, we are told so; she is witty, we know her to be so. Her wit, like all good wit, can be mischievous. Portia enjoys mocking at the peculiarities of her suitors and deliberately invites Nerissa to 'over-name' them, so that she can amuse herself by recounting their eccentricities. For all her success as a doctor of law she is supremely feminine in this, as well as in her teasing of Bassanio over the lost ring. What are we to make of her character? A young, beautiful, witty girl, who must live in perpetual fear of being married to a Neapolitan prince who resembles a horse, a weeping Palatine count, a simpering French lord, a dolt of an Englishman, a quarrelling Scotsman, a drunken German, a black-a-moor Moroccan, or a really quite impossible gentleman from Arragon. Is this witty and cultured heiress really prepared to accept a husband whose sole claim to her heart is the fact that he chooses a lead casket? Has this woman, who is capable of outwitting the cunning Jew, no will of her own? Does she, perhaps, load the dice by hinting which casket her suitors should choose? To do so would be to suspect her honesty, for she swears she will die as chaste as Diana unless she be obtained by the manner of her father's will. And her father has decreed that only he who chooses the right casket shall inherit his daughter and her fabulous fortune.

The critics who declare this story of the caskets to be boring argue that everyone in the audience knows that Bassanio will choose the lead casket, and therefore the casket scenes lack dramatic tension. I can only reply that everyone in the audience knows that Cinderella's foot will fit the glass slipper. The producers who introduce such tricks as turning the song 'Tell me where is fancy bred' into a subtle innuendo that 'lead' which rhymes with 'bred' is the right choice, or who introduce various oglings and pointings from Nerissa and Portia to indicate to Bassanio which casket he should choose, show a complete ignorance of the simplicity of a fairy story and forget how we can still be charmed by a land of make-belief. Let us please not destroy the poetry of the casket scenes by sniggerings and hints in a futile attempt to make the story naturalistic. The magic of the theatre does not depend only on suspense, and there is as much good theatre in a pantomime as there is in Ibsen. Belmont is and must remain a land where fancy is bred. Let us make it a fairy tale country with its sweet music, its moonlit banks, its ceremonious processions of suitors to Portia's hand and its simple but moving tale of the caskets.

Morocco and Arragon

What of the outlandish suitors who come to make their choice? Morocco is often represented as a comic figure, but I think this is unfair to him and to Shakespeare's verse. As with the Shylock-Antonio situation, we have in the wooing of Portia by Morocco another form of the racial problem. Shakespeare was clearly concerned with the question of mixed marriage and dealt with it at greater length in *Othello*, but whereas he is prepared to vilify the Jew he seems to be sympathetic to the question of the coloured races. Nothing is more indicative of character than reaction to failure, and in the true English style Shakespeare shows his characters' temper by the way they behave when they fail. Morocco takes the umpire's decision like a good cricketer:

'Portia, adieu. I have too grieved a heart
To take a tedious leave: thus lovers part.'

We must conclude from his courteous behaviour and the majesty of his lines that the Prince of Morocco is a gentleman. With Arragon it is different; when he loses he shows bad temper, or at least petulance:

'Still more fool I shall appear
By the time I linger here:
With one fool's head I came to woo,
But I go away with two.
Sweet, adieu: I'll keep my oath
Patiently to bear my wroth.'

We have, therefore, a right to regard Arragon as a pompous,

self-satisfied prig, thoroughly deserving his reward—the portrait of a blinking idiot.

Balthasar and Stephano

I would like to say one word about Portia's servants. Balthasar is responsible for arranging Portia's flight and seems to be her steward. As such I want him played with something of the mannered courtesy which will warrant Portia's remark to him—'What would my lord?' As her steward he is responsible for the ceremonious arrangements for the choosing of the caskets. Stephano is ordered to bring his music forth into the air, so we must presume him to be responsible for the music in Portia's household. I propose to make him into a zany, the sort of half-witted plaything who follows his mistress around like a dog, only half comprehending what is being said to her, but intensely conscious of her moods, rejoicing in her happiness with Bassanio, terrified of Morocco and Arragon. In this way he will reflect Portia's anxiety over the choice of the caskets and will help to build up the Arcadian atmosphere of the fairy tale island.

The Jews

Although we have examined Shylock's position in the play, there remains the question of his background and family life which is important, in that it concerns his daughter's elopement and his own determination to press for his revenge. We have seen how the Venetians are divided into the social groups of merchants and gentlemen; equally we must consider the racial grouping of Shylock, Tubal and Jessica. To-day the Jewish communities outside Israel have on the surface been largely absorbed into the customs and habits of their adopted countries, but in the Renaissance age they remained a distinctive community preserving not only their religious and social apartness, but also their native habits and costume. The Jews are Orientals, rather than Occidentals, and lean more to the East than to the Roman world. So we would expect to find Shylock, Jessica and Tubal dressed in a fashion which is nearer to Persia than to London. By making this distinction of dress we are able to bring about a complete change in Jessica when she goes over to the Christian way of life, and emphasize that, when Shylock is instructed to turn Christian, he is in fact not only required to change his religion, but to change his clothes, and with them his behaviour and his whole way of living. The Orientalism of the Jews is emphasized by two scenes in the text: firstly, the scene in which Shylock shows his patriarchal attitude towards Jessica, bidding her lock herself close within the house (Act II, Sc. 5); secondly, the scene between Tubal and Shylock (Act III, Sc. 1) where Tubal appears to be deliberately provoking his fellow-countryman to madness. In fact, Tubal is a rival money-lender and however sympathetic he may feel towards the misfortunes of Shylock, he cannot resist the Oriental pleasure of seeing Shylock writhe beneath the whip of misfortune, nor can he forgo the pleasure of driving Shylock onwards as an instrument of racial revenge. Both Tubal and Shylock are professional money-lenders, and to the Jew as to the Oriental money-lending is a legitimate trade, sanctioned in the Jewish case by biblical authority. Thus for both of them Antonio, by his practice of lending out money gratis, is deliberately and wrongfully undermining their trade. It is an integral part of the Jewish way of life to make money and to thrive through cunning; this is no less true of other Oriental races such as the Egyptians and the Persians. To undermine usury is to undermine religion: 'You take my house when you do take the prop that doth sustain my house; you take my life when you do take the means whereby I live'. It is not just the taking of his money from him that hurts, but the injustice of imposing upon one race the morality and customs of another. This distinction of cultures can be emphasized by providing Shylock, Jessica and Tubal with the sort of Oriental costume which separates them from the Europeans.

The Gobbos

The last of the social groups which make up the characters of the play is that of the Gobbos, father and son. These are the low comedy elements which Shakespeare provides to contrast with the high comedy elements of his lovers. Launcelot is, as we know, Shylock's servant; as such his place in the early part of the play is to keep that dangerously human villain in his place as a villain. Shylock seen by us through Launcelot is a miserly and thoroughly unattractive master—'the very devil himself'—from whose service Launcelot is justified in escaping. Launcelot's sole regret at leaving Shylock is that he has to part from the Jew's beautiful daughter, with whom he has a sympathy bred of mutual suffering. Thus beyond Launcelot's task of providing low comedy relief, there is the secondary, but no less important task, of enhancing Jessica's reputation and of condemning her cruel and tyrannical father. Once his task as a pillar of the play's construction is finished, Shakespeare wisely exiles him to Belmont, where his cheerful fooling can do no harm to the serious business of the trial.

The Trial Scene

This is the serious business of the fairy story. I have emphasized that the lovers are fairy story people, because they have so often been mistaken for the contrary, but every fairy story must have its drama and *The Merchant* is no exception. The trial scene is too well known to require much analysis, but I would draw your attention to two things; firstly, the skill with which Portia conducts her case, and secondly, the dramatic coup-de-théatre with which she wins it.

Portia comes to the court uncertain of the outcome. There must be no suggestion, if we are to maintain the tension of the scene, that she knows she is going to win. She has learned from the lawyer, Bellario, certain scraps of Venetian law relative to aliens and citizens—such as the fact that if an alien seeks the life of a Venetian, his goods are confiscate—she has also learned that a bond legally entered into cannot be broken by any power in Venice. Legally, therefore, the Jew can claim his pound of flesh:

> 'Why this bond is forfeit,
> And lawfully by this the Jew may claim
> A pound of flesh . . .'

Bellario has told her the only hopes of saving Antonio depend, firstly, on the faint possibility that the bond has been badly drawn up—has any allowance been made for shedding human blood? And, secondly, on the possibility that Shylock himself has overstepped the law. If, for instance, Shylock has brought, or is prepared to bring, a surgeon into the court—however useless that individual would be under the circumstances—then Shylock cannot be accused of a deliberate attempt on a Venetian's life. If he has failed to do so, then he is guilty of attempted murder and the law can penalize him. But it would be extremely unwise for Portia to count on either of these possibilities. Every means must first be explored before testing such possible chinks. Portia starts her case by asking if Antonio confesses the bond. He replies that he does. Legally, therefore, the case is lost. There remains the possibility of an infringement by Shylock or a badly drawn up agreement. She appeals to the Jew for mercy, not that she expects him to comply, but because she must have time to assess her opponent, and since her case now rests on possible, but improbable, circumstances, she must first try every means open to her, other than the law. Lastly, she will try to draw the sympathy of the court to her client and against Shylock. If he refuses to show mercy then he, at least, cannot expect to receive a sympathetic hearing even if his case is sound. Next she tries to induce him to give up his case by playing on his well-known greed for money. Having tried these two methods of conciliation and having failed, Portia realizes that she must have recourse to the faint possibility that a mistake has been made by the notary who drew up the agreement. She asks to see the bond. Having read it, she suddenly realizes that in his haste for revenge the Jew has overlooked the details. There is no mention of blood. Now she knows Antonio to be safe, she can proceed to test the second possibility which, if it turns out to be true, will turn Shylock into a criminal. She makes an appeal to Shylock to show mercy by asking him to have by some surgeon to stop the flow of blood. When Shylock refuses this and when the knife is poised over Antonio's breast, Portia suddenly turns the tables on the Jew. He can have the flesh, but not a drop of blood. The scraps of Venetian law she has gleaned from Bellario fall into place: the law insists that to attempt to take a Venetian's life is a crime; had Shylock agreed to the presence of a surgeon and to taking all reasonable precautions to prevent Antonio's death, he would have left the court a free man, but his greedy desire for revenge has lost him more than his case. Why then does Portia delay the point and allow Antonio and Bassanio the agony of their final farewell? Because she must wait until the knife is actually poised over Antonio before she can claim that this alien is intending to kill a Venetian. Only when that act is undeniably proved is Shylock guilty of a crime against the state. During these last few minutes, between the realization of her success and the raising of the knife, Portia can afford to relax and be amused over Bassanio's offer to give up his wife to save Antonio's life.

This sudden realization by Portia of how to defeat Shylock is not only important theatrically, but also from the point of view of Portia's integrity; for if Portia is to come into court knowing from the beginning that she can save Antonio, then how can we regard her as other than a sadistic young lady who deliberately prolongs the agony of her husband's friend in order to win personal renown.

Of course we must agree that there is a fairy tale element about all this, otherwise how do Bassanio and Gratiano fail to recognize Portia and Nerissa when they are dressed as men? I don't think there is any need for desperate attempts to disguise Portia and her maid, other than by their male costume, for this make-believe atmosphere adds its own touch of lightness to an otherwise purely dramatic scene, helping to keep the play within the realms of 'once upon a time'.

The Last Scene

To finish the fairy story we are led back to Belmont for the last scene. The villain has been defeated, the honest merchant rescued, and it remains only to round off this tale by uniting the lovers. After the grim story of the pound of flesh and the degrading sight of the cringing Jew, here is magic itself. The little pavilion rises, the lights change to darkness and shadows, above us are the stars. There standing in a shaft of moonlight are Jessica and Lorenzo gazing out in wonder at the splendour of the night:

> 'In such a night as this,
> When the sweet wind did gently kiss the trees,
> And they did make no noise . . .'

and then come Portia and Nerissa to lean against the pillars and listen to the hymn to Diana; then their lovers, and by the light of the moon the raillery of the ring scene seems like the mating-dance of peacocks or the midnight gambols of March hares in the season of wooing. The females pirouette and decline the advances of the males, but at last they give way. As the first perfumes of the morning air rise, the little procession of lovers with Antonio moves off to answer all things faithfully. So the cover of the story book is closed and we creep upstairs to bed with the music and the poetry of this last scene lingering in our ears, forgetting if we can the lonely shadow of the broken outcast creeping back to his empty home.

POSTSCRIPT

How far should a producer be influenced by his critics? There is a type of theatre critic who believes his mission in life is to reform Shakespearian production. Producers of Shakespeare, argues this missionary, are purveyors of trivial frivolities; their desire is to load the production with useless processions and dances, with busy comings and goings; they care nothing for the verse of the play and bury the actors beneath fuss, flutter and frizz. There is, of course, some truth in all this and the producer of Shakespeare must be constantly critical of excesses of imagination, whether they be his own, the actor's or the designer's. But the danger of such puritan zealots is, that they push their arguments too far in an effort to ridicule the object of their aversion.

The producer would not be human if he was oblivious to criticism and he would be insensitive if he was not hurt by it. The danger is that he should be intimidated by it. Once his mind is fettered by the fear of providing this or that critic with an opportunity of riding his hobby-horse, his production will no longer be his own. The critic, too, is but human. His notice has to be built around some positive angle. If he is criticizing a new play, he can and does criticize the play itself, but no critic can turn in an adverse criticism of Shakespeare to his editor, even if he would dearly like to. His angle then must be found in the performance.

The actors are fair game, but since the critic is never sure of the dividing line between acting and production, and, since it seems rather unfair to wound the actor who has to continue to play the part night after night, the critic prefers to go for the producer. All this is fair enough and the producer, if he is wise, will lick his sores and prefer to criticize himself.

The Merchant of Venice received an exceedingly flattering press except from one of the puritans, who used it—unfairly I think—as an opportunity to ride his hobby-horse. Now this play presents the producer with a difficulty. It is somewhat hackneyed; it carries with it memories of school performances in draughty halls and of readings by Shakespearian circles. The producer's job is to restore its magic. In doing this he knows that the puritan will cry for less production, but his task is to lead the audience to an enjoyment of the play. If he does this, and remains true to his author, he has succeeded.

JULIUS CAESAR

JULIUS CAESAR
Old Vic Theatre
24th February 1953

FLAVIUS	PATRICK WYMARK
FIRST CITIZEN	BRUCE SHARMAN
MARULLUS	DANIEL THORNDIKE
SECOND CITIZEN	GEORGE MURCELL
JULIUS CAESAR	DOUGLAS CAMPBELL
CASCA	WILLIAM SQUIRE
CALPURNIA	YVONNE COULETTE
MARK ANTONY	ROBIN BAILEY
A SOOTHSAYER	WOLFE MORRIS
BRUTUS	WILLIAM DEVLIN
CASSIUS	PAUL ROGERS
CICERO	NEWTON BLICK
CINNA	JAMES MAXWELL
LUCIUS	TERRY WALE
DECIUS BRUTUS	JOHN WARNER
METELLUS CIMBER	DANIEL THORNDIKE
TREBONIUS	PATRICK WYMARK
PORTIA	HELEN CHERRY
SERVANT TO CAESAR	BERNARD KILBY
PUBLIUS	BRUCE SHARMAN
ARTEMIDORUS	PERCY HERBERT
POPILIUS LENA	EUGENE LEAHY
SERVANT TO ANTONY	TONY VAN BRIDGE
SERVANT TO OCTAVIUS	DENIS RAYMOND
CINNA THE POET	JOHN WARNER
OCTAVIUS CAESAR	DOUGLAS CAMPBELL

[Photograph: Desmond Tripp, Bristol]

'This was the noblest Roman of them all'

(*Above*) OCTAVIUS: Douglas Campbell (*Below*) BRUTUS: William Devlin

MARK ANTONY: Robin Bailey

[Photograph: Desmond Tripp, Bristol

The Tent Scene

CASSIUS: Paul Rogers   TITINIUS: Percy Herbert
BRUTUS: William Devlin   MASSALA: Tony van Bridge

[Photograph: Desmond Tripp, Bristol

The curtain should fall on the flames of a burning Rome as they flicker on
the mangled limbs of the first of many victims of the dogs of civil war

LEPIDUS	TONY VAN BRIDGE
LUCILIUS	NEWTON BLICK
PINDARUS	WOLFE MORRIS
MESSALA	TONY VAN BRIDGE
VARRO	BERNARD KILBY
CLAUDIUS	JAMES MAXWELL
MESSENGER TO ANTONY	DOUGLAS RAIN
TITINIUS	PERCY HERBERT
YOUNG CATO	ALAN DOBIE
CLITUS	PATRICK WYMARK
DARDANIUS	BRUCE SHARMAN
VOLUMNIUS	DANIEL THORNDIKE
STRATO	GEORGE MURCELL

CITIZENS, SOLDIERS, SENATORS, CENTURIONS, ETC.:
GARTH ADAMS, PETER AUGUSTINE, JOHN BEARY, DAVID BENSON, DENZIL ELLIS, NORMAN FRASER, PHILIP GALE, PAT HORGAN, ALAN JOHN, GERALD LIMBRECK, JOHAN MALHERBE, HENRY MARA, DESMOND RAYNER, JOHN STOCKBRIDGE, ERIC THOMPSON, BARBARA GRIMES, PHYLLIDA LAW.

Scenery by Tanya Moiseiwitsch. Costumes by Alan Tagg. Music composed by Christopher Whelan.

JULIUS CAESAR

IN tackling the history of *Julius Caesar*, Shakespeare was on dangerous ground, for the death of that hero of antiquity was a subject familiar to every London schoolboy, infinitely more so than the histories of *Richard III* or *King John*. Shakespeare had no great background of classical scholarship on which to draw, and in dealing with such a subject he could not allow his imagination to soar into the realms of fancy; for, if fooling around with English history was permissible, such treatment applied to the subject of Julius Caesar would be strongly resented in an age when reverence for Roman virtues was a basis of culture.

The story of Caesar's death was too well known both by scholar and apprentice-boy to allow any considerable liberty to be taken with history, and Shakespeare was forced to follow faithfully the textbook most readily available to him, namely North's translation of *Plutarch's Lives*. The result is that in *Julius Caesar* we have a dramatization of a history book, in which incidents are sometimes included more for reasons of historical fact than for dramatic value. It is, of course, a fact that Shakespeare took all his plays from one source or another, and his English histories were also based on historical textbooks. But in the English histories he allows himself wide latitude for invention, in *Julius Caesar* he follows his source with extreme caution. We might call this slavish subservience to the historians were it not for the fact that his sense of theatre and his magnificent rhetoric enriches most, but not all, of the adapted incidents. The tent scene, for instance, in which Brutus and Cassius quarrel, an incident fully related by Plutarch, adds nothing to the development of the plot, nor does it tell us anything new about these two characters, but without this scene as transformed by Shakespeare, the play would be infinitely the poorer. Again in the murder of Cinna the Poet, which Shakespeare lifts straight out of Plutarch, he is merely reporting an incident which is extraneous to the dramatic action, and yet with what skill does he convert this extraneous incident into a terrifying condemnation of mob violence and revolution.

There are, however, other incidents taken directly from the history book which are less happy. The arrival of the sick conspirator Ligarius after the conspirators' scene seems pointless, nor has he been successful in treating the incident of the eccentric poet in the tent scene, whilst the profusion of suicides in the last act sets a serious problem to the producer of to-day, who is aware of the danger of the schoolboy's giggle at this point of the play. The reverence for Roman history, held in such regard by the Elizabethans, seems to have somewhat cramped Shakespeare's imagination and perhaps deterred him from introducing any comic relief into his play. As a result the characters tend to move on a plane of unrelieved nobility, which can be a little boring for a modern audience who do not share the Renaissance enthusiasm for Roman heroics. But if Shakespeare thought it unseemly to have any Warwickshire clowns wandering around the Capitol, he was able to introduce, through the medium of the crowd, an earthy element to balance the less digestible portions of Romanism. This play is unrelieved by comedy, but it is shot through with the ironic laughter of the gods, an irony which becomes apparent as we see the idealistic dreams of the noble-minded conspirators tumbling down about their ears, and as the removal of one tyranny brings a worse tyranny in its place.

Now here we begin to touch on what the play is about. *Julius Caesar* is clearly a history play, a dramatization of Caesar's death, and as such I maintain that the central character is Julius Caesar and not Brutus or Mark Antony. I do not mean that Caesar is the hero of the play, for he dies half-way through and he does not take part in the progress of the action, except as a reason for other people's action. What I mean is that Caesar is the central symbol of the play, and that is why the play is called *Julius Caesar* and not *Brutus* or *Mark Antony* or *Cassius*. It is true that Caesar himself has little to say, but his influence pervades the story and never more strongly than after his death. This production of the play therefore aims at centralizing the character of Caesar and keeping alive the symbolism of this central character until the curtain falls.

If Caesar's murder is the subject of the play, what are we meant to learn from it? Are we intended to see in it a sympathetic view of the Roman general, or the principle of monarchy as opposed to republicanism? Or is it a play glorifying Brutus and vilifying Mark Antony? Is Caesar's death a crime or is Brutus's death a tragedy? Surely the audience must sympathize with one side or the other in a battle between such distinct and important political opposites. Let us quickly glance at the principal protagonists and what they stand for. In so far as there is a hero of this play, then that hero is Brutus. He is portrayed throughout as a man of honour who dies with his honour unscathed. Antony, it is true, claims our admiration by his brilliant feat of turning the tables on the conspirators and our respect by his loyalty to Caesar. He has more charm than Brutus, more warmth, more sense of adventure, but his unscrupulousness turns our sympathies away from him and back to Brutus.

As a human being Cassius is more interesting than either, and as a character he is more subtly drawn. Moreover, despite his very human faults, or perhaps because of them, we feel more sorry for him than for Brutus. But Brutus is the noble Roman, the high-minded idealist who, like Hamlet, takes upon himself at the call of duty a deed which is repugnant to his nature. But it is this deed which matters and in this deed, namely the assassination of the Roman dictator, lies the heart as well as the subject matter of the play.

Before we examine the rights or wrongs of Caesar's murder, let us digress for a moment into historical matters which

Shakespeare has not expressly mentioned, but about which he had undoubtedly read and thought. It is, as a rule, a dangerous practice for a producer or an actor to look elsewhere than at the text of a play for a source of characterization, more especially is this true in Shakespeare's historical plays. It can lead the players into the error of representing history as it really was, instead of history as it is conceived by the playwright; and there is often a vast difference between the two. In this instance an investigation of history as Shakespeare knew it is justified, since in *Julius Caesar* the playwright stuck rigidly to his textbook, only departing from it for good dramatic reasons.

Let us briefly look at the historical Caesar as related by Plutarch and see why and how Shakespeare departed from his model. The Rome of Caesar's youth was no longer the stoic city-state of Romulus and Remus. The effects of a highly developed standard of living; central heating, main drainage, unrationed orgies, somewhat over-produced revues in the Colosseum and spectacular triumphs through the streets had a little lowered the high moral tone of Roman virtues. Roman Society was decidedly decadent; the purity of Roman citizenship had been dragged down by the pernicious system of slavery; the great patrician families had lost their position of leadership and their ranks were contaminated by intermarriage with the rising class of unscrupulous middlemen. Politics had become a matter of bribery and corruption and the religion of the ancient gods had descended into a pure formality which played no part in the moral or social outlook of the citizen.

At an early age Caesar developed a desire for power and a scorn for the existing state of affairs. But he quickly realized that the jealously guarded Roman constitution would not allow power to be invested in any single man for long enough to allow him to effect reforms. The highest position in the state, the Consulship, was a dual office and had to be shared with a fellow Consul. It was only an annual appointment and thus any major reforms were exceedingly difficult to put into practice. To amalgamate the various political parties and achieve a more permanent power over the Senate's policy required, if not statesmanship of a high order, at least a great deal of money. Caesar, like Pompey and others before him, realized that the quickest way to achieve power lay in the possession of an army loyal to their general rather than to Rome.

After reaching high office in the state he was appointed to a military command and set forth on those campaigns with which he has ever since plagued every schoolboy's life, and during the course of which he conquered the world. Caesar was a great tourist and an intelligent one. He not only conquered the then known world, but he allowed himself to be absorbed by it. He put to good use the customs and laws of other peoples, and turned himself into a great administrator as well as a great general. From time to time he returned to Rome to act as Consul and with him he brought new ideas and fresh life to the city. He might have been content to continue as the architect of the Roman Empire rather than the ruler of the Roman capital had not his friends seen in him the instrument of their own political ambitions, and persuaded him to cross the Rubicon with an army at his back and advance on Rome. Having overcome Pompey, his only serious rival, Caesar was master of the city. He was given much power and honour and the title of dictator. But Caesar was dissatisfied. The Rome to which he returned was still the same corrupt, smug, self-satisfied city. Accustomed as he was to the variegated and fascinating life of the Empire, to the genuine homage and respect which he commanded abroad, he was barely able to veil his contempt for the narrow-minded intrigue of the Roman factions, who regarded Rome as the only city and the Roman law as the only law. He threw off all pretences of republican practice, paraded the streets like a king, threw open the privileges of Roman citizenship to the barbarians whom he had conquered, invited Cleopatra and a huge retinue to visit him in Rome, received the Senators sitting down, and was planning to be crowned Imperator if not of Rome itself, at least of the Roman world outside. No doubt he felt it would increase his prestige when visiting the vassal monarchs of his empire if he had some mighty handle to his name; if he were called Roman Emperor rather than Roman General. How often can this question of a title be the turning point of a great man's life? Did not the same moment arrive when Cromwell became Lord Protector, Napoleon Emperor of the French, Mussolini Il Duce, and Hitler the Fuehrer? How many times does the dictator type change from being a great statesman, military leader or reformer, into a tyrant at this very point of his career, when he finally throws off all pretence at modesty and gives vent to his egoism by assuming one of these high-sounding titles.

Caesar was slain by the conspirators at that very turning point and we shall never know whether Caesar would have become a tyrant or not. We shall therefore never know whether Brutus's fears were justified. For note that Shakespeare makes Brutus kill Caesar not for what he was, nor for what he had done, but for what he might become:—

> 'And, since, the quarrel
> Will bear no colour for the thing he is,
> Fashion it thus; *that what he is, augmented,*
> *Would run to these and these extremities:*
> And therefore think him as a serpent's egg,
> Which, hatch'd, would as his kind grown mischievous.'

Shakespeare has been accused of deliberately debasing the character of Caesar, of making him a shadow of the historical man. I am sure that to belittle Caesar or to caricature him was very far from Shakespeare's intention. The Elizabethans held Roman history in high reverence and every Elizabethan schoolboy knew the reasons why Caesar could claim to be one of the world's great men. Shakespeare was not so foolish as to attempt to reverse the deep-seated prejudices of his audience in so summary a fashion. If he makes no attempt to lay stress upon Caesar's qualities, it is because Caesar's qualities were generally known. What he is concerned about is to explain why Brutus and his fellow conspirators thought fit to kill Caesar, and to make their motive plausible and strong. He, therefore, shows Julius Caesar at the turning point of his career when greatness may turn to tyranny, the serpent's egg which, hatch'd, would grow mischievous. His audience knew that Caesar was great, but what they could not be expected to know was, that Caesar showed signs of falling from grace.

It is the actor's task to represent Caesar at that precise moment when a fine mind might reasonably be expected to turn to the madness of egoism. It is not what Caesar says that shows us Caesar, but the position he already occupies in the audience's knowledge and the influence he wields over the other characters. Shakespeare's real problem was not how to portray Caesar, but how to deal with the conspirators. His dramatic task required him to explain Caesar's murder, and to do this he had first to build up sympathy for, or at any rate an understanding of, the anti-Caesar faction without which the whole play would have been unbalanced. The skill with which he does in fact balance his material has been misunderstood by most of his commentators, who have seized on the brief appearances of the character of Caesar and the pomposity and superstition of his utterances without taking into account, firstly, the audience's knowledge of Caesar and, secondly, the brilliant way in which the character is built up to heroic proportions after the murder has taken place. For once the audience has accepted the conspirators as men motivated by idealism rather than as base assassins; once Brutus is established and Cassius understood, then Shakespeare can safely allow the pendulum to swing towards the Caesar faction in the person of Antony, who up to that moment is kept discreetly in the background. And how quickly this pendulum does swing! Caesar dead becomes the people's benefactor, whilst Brutus and Cassius are thrown into confusion and the cause they espoused begins to crumble beneath their feet, even as Antony utters that terrifying prophecy:

> 'And Caesar's spirit ranging for revenge
> With Ate by his side, come hot from hell,
> Shall in these confines, with a monarch's voice,
> Cry "Havoc" and let slip the dogs of war . . .'

The Roman citizens, for whose benefit this deed of liberation was performed, become a leaderless mob who ruthlessly burn their city and murder innocent people. And Brutus who struck down his friend and benefactor to save the citizens from Caesar is ironically hailed by them as a second Caesar. So is confusion heaped upon confusion and civil war rends asunder the city which the liberators had sought to save from tyranny. Then, too, do the chief conspirators begin to break up; Brutus is visited by visions, Cassius is accused of financial extortion, Brutus's judgement is twice proved faulty, whilst Cassius in a moment of over-hasty despair slays himself.

The confusion and chaos which overtake the conspirators and their cause have a reason behind them, and the reason is the attitude to the play for which we are searching. The removal of Caesar, although idealistically motivated, was not justifiable. It was achieved by revolution, and revolution which lets slip the unbridled frenzy of the rabble is a wrongful action jeopardizing the delicately balanced structure of society. To Shakespeare human society—as represented by the social scale of sovereign, nobles, church and people—was a precious possession to be guarded at all costs. We sometimes accuse Shakespeare of being against the people, of being autocratic in his political sympathies. We are perhaps forgetful of the times in which he lived. We have to-day a reasonably responsible attitude towards the state. Political assassination and incitement of the less responsible elements to burn, murder and kill are frowned upon by our more responsible politicians, even when they have failed to win a general election. But in the Elizabethan age such an attitude was a comparative novelty. The whole era from the death of Henry VIII to the accession of Elizabeth had been one of continual civil turbulence. Even under Elizabeth the state had been strained and threatened by foreign intrigues and by continual threats of insurrection. The responsible citizens of London, amongst whom Shakespeare lived, knew how easily their well-ordered state could be shaken, how apprentice boys could be roused by a skilful orator and how houses could be burned down, wives and daughters raped and themselves clubbed in the streets. It is this fearful monster of mass revolution that Shakespeare decries in *Julius Caesar*. 'Cry "Havoc" and let slip the dogs of war'—that is the crime of Brutus, the conspirators and indeed of Mark Antony.

Moreover, Caesar was not in fact guilty of any crime against the state as yet. The argument used by Brutus, namely that Caesar's murder might be justified by events which might have occurred had Caesar been allowed to live, is neither sound in human law nor in any court of moral justice. So it comes about that Nemesis overtakes the conspirators and their guilt can only be washed away by their blood. Shakespeare asks his audience to understand, but not to condone, the reasons for eliminating Caesar. He asks them to accept the deaths of Brutus and Cassius as a necessary punishment for the sin of overthrowing the government by violence.

Thus this play is about revolution which, however idealistically motivated, is an unjustifiable act. Shakespeare does not wish to hold Julius Caesar up to us as a model of government, indeed he has taken pains to expose his weakness in order to balance his play. Caesar is not the hero of the play. He is, however, the symbol of stable government and no man, however ideal his motives, has the right to overthrow stable government by force, unless that government as in *Richard II*, *Richard III* and *Macbeth* is manifestly incapable of assuring order or is in itself evil. Caesar, then, is the symbol of stable government, and even if he might become a tyrant, he is not yet guilty. His overthrow is, therefore, unjustifiable.

You may argue that it is only a history play and that since these events actually happened Shakespeare gave the play no special pattern of his own. Perhaps that is true, perhaps history has a pattern; if that is so, then it is the playwright's task to clarify that pattern and present it in dramatic terms. Whether Shakespeare extracted this pattern out of the history book or whether he imposed it on the facts does not matter; it is clear that he deliberately suppressed historical facts which would endanger the clarity of the pattern in which he believed. Up to the moment of Caesar's death, he follows Plutarch closely and at times slavishly. But once the historical incident has been truthfully recorded, he plays Old Harry with history in order to drive home his point. The war between Antony and Octavius prior to their joint campaign is totally disregarded. Roman politics are thrown to the winds, Brutus's mysterious visitor, whom Plutarch only describes as an evil omen, is deliberately changed by Shakespeare into the ghost of Caesar, and finally the idea of purgation for a wrongful act is pointed home by the deaths of Brutus and Cassius. So Cassius:

'. . . and with this good sword
That ran through Caesar's bowels, search this bosom.'

So Brutus over Cassius's body:

'. . . O Julius Caesar, thou art mighty yet,
Thy spirit walks abroad, and turns our swords
In our own proper entrails.'

So Brutus at his own death:

'. . . Caesar, now be still,
I kill'd not thee with half so good a will.'

So much then for our approach to the pattern of this play which starts by deliberately leading us to think the conspirators are right and then shows us how tragically wrong they were.

Now for the characters themselves. First, let us say that Shakespeare is at pains to show us Romans, not Englishmen. In the age of the Renaissance the Romans were regarded as an altogether higher order of beings to the representatives of any other age of mankind; so, although he represented ancient Britons or the court of Theseus and Hippolyta in much the same way as he represented the Venetians in *The Merchant of Venice*, or the Illyrians in *Twelfth Night*; although Dogberry could find his way to Messina and Bottom to Athens, such liberties were not to be taken with the high Roman order. The characteristics of this Renaissance conception of the Roman order were: firstly, that everyone should act remarkably nobly; secondly, that the players of these superior beings should make frequent invocation to the spirit of their ancestors, and every now and then thump their chests exclaiming 'O ye Gods'; and thirdly, that as many as possible should kill themselves by running on their swords. This is what the Elizabethan audience expected of their Roman plays and this is what Shakespeare and Burbage had to give them.

Julius Caesar

I believe it is entirely wrong to caricature Caesar's eccentricities. Shakespeare has pointed the danger of Caesar's egoitism, it is not the actor's job to exaggerate it. Caesar is a Colossus. He knows more about life than anyone else in the play, he is tired of pretending he is a mere Roman citizen, tired of the people, their ignorance, their stinking breath; he is bored with men like Cassius who read and observe too much. He knows that people intrigue behind his back and above all he knows that, if they remove him, they have nothing concrete to put in his place—for Caesar is the state. He is courageous; he would rather die suddenly than wait for death to come to him. In the meantime he will not compromise, for he knows that he is the greatest man on earth and he cannot be bothered to disguise the fact. He has reached the summit of man's ambition and found the top of the mountain singularly barren. He could save Rome if Rome wanted to be saved, but lacking any personal humility he cannot stoop to save it. Despising the intellectual idealists, he prefers Antony with his love of games and plays, his laughter and his love of music. He has become intolerant and impatient; if Rome will not accept him, then he will establish the seat of Empire elsewhere, accept the crown and start a new Rome in Macedonia or Egypt—such was his threat. There is, however, one weakness in this Colossus—his superstition (remember that both Wallenstein and Hitler had their fortune-tellers). It is not that Caesar fears death, but he fears the way in which death might come to him. He has seen too many men die to fear it, but he wants to make history and die nobly, not to be stabbed in the back and show himself a coward. Well, history relates that he was stabbed in the back; but for all that he died nobly, fighting like a lion in the Senate House until he met Brutus's dagger. Then the fight went out of him; Brutus, whom he had loved as a son had allowed himself to be tricked into joining the ranks of Caesar's enemies. There was no more to say, no reason to prolong the fight:

'Et tu, Brute? Then fall, Caesar!'

But the man who fell lived on, and the proud prophecy of his assassins—

'How many ages hence shall this our lofty scene be acted over, in states unborn and accents yet unknown.'

proved true, only the greatness crowned not Brutus or Cassius, but Julius Caesar.

Brutus

Although the central character of the play is Caesar, the hero of it is Brutus. An unsatisfactory hero, I maintain, since not even Shakespeare's magic can wholly persuade us to like this humourless character. We must not mistakenly imagine that this revolutionary leader was a son of the soil, nor confuse him with the heroes of Marxian mythology. Brutus like most revolutionary leaders and philosophers was a patrician; more of a nobleman in fact than Caesar himself. He traced his ancestry back to the earliest Romans and for this reason he was persuaded by Cassius that his duty lay in defending the republican movement, which his ancestors had helped to create.

Shakespeare had, I think, some personal difficulty in dramatizing Brutus. He realized to the full Brutus's integrity, his stoicism, his sense of honour, but I also believe he preferred Antony, whose appeal was less intellectual. In dramatizing the part of Brutus Shakespeare was fighting his way towards Hamlet, but his material in terms of history was less pliable, it did not allow him the same liberty nor the same humanity as he was able to infuse into the character of Hamlet. Brutus is a philosopher, an idealist who fears Caesar's nature, but who loves him as a man. He is led by a sense of duty to kill Caesar, discovering too late his mistake and acknowledging it by his own death. All these facts are in his favour, and command his author's sympathy, but Brutus is a prig, he is always telling us how honourable he is, and this high sense of honour leads him to make fatally unrealistic decisions.

If history did not help Shakespeare to make a human being

of Brutus, imagination came to his aid on at least three telling occasions, when he managed to humanize this rather unpliable material. The first is in the scene with Portia, a woman who is both a Roman matron and a wife in love with her husband; the second is in the quarrel between Cassius and Brutus which brings out the heart of Brutus; and the third is by the attitude of the common soldiers towards Brutus, in which we see the love that Brutus could command and the humanity that he could show towards simple people. Shakespeare has given Brutus three supreme moments; his scene with Portia, his tent scene following the quarrel when he suddenly descends from his pedestal to tell Cassius of Portia's death, and lastly his own death scene, when, like a lost soul in search of salvation, he seeks for a friendly hand to help him to end it all. None of these is strictly historical and each shows Shakespeare penetrating the rather intractable marble of the historical Brutus and making it live. To end it all he explains Brutus to us in Antony's final oration:

'This was the noblest Roman of them all,
All the conspirators, save only he,
Did that they did in envy of great Caesar:
He, only, in a general honest thought,
And common good to all, made one of them.
His life was gentle, and the elements
So mix'd in him, that Nature might stand up
And say to all the world, "This was a man".'

The actor who plays Brutus must beware of emphasizing the prig and this can best be done by underlining the gentleness of the man, his quiet assurance, once his mind is made up, his love for Portia, for Lucius and for the common soldiers, and his complete lack of bitterness for, or envy of, his enemies.

Cassius

Cassius I have claimed to be the most interesting character in the play. His motives are less noble than those of Brutus. Unlike the latter he was envious of Caesar, and in sowing the seed of revolution he was not entirely free of that sin. Why should Caesar be—

> '. . . now become a god? He had a fever when he was in Spain,
> and when the fit was on him, I did mark how he did shake!'

On another occasion Caesar called on Cassius to save him from the waves of Tiber. What has Caesar got that Cassius has not? Well, we know, but it is painfully hard to explain it to Cassius, without hurting his feelings, for Cassius is most easily hurt. Caesar is a Colossus compared with Cassius, and yet Cassius is more lovable than Caesar. He is no leader; he is not even strictly honourable, for he has recourse to dishonest means to raise funds for the republican army; moreover, he lacks stability. When he sees Popilius Lena approach Caesar in the Senate he is on the point of throwing in his hand and committing suicide at the crucial moment. These waves of despair which are a result of his sudden moods lead him on another occasion to threaten Brutus and on yet another to slay himself on the field of Philippi. He is burdened with a quick temper, he is said by Shakespeare, not by Plutarch, to love no plays nor music and to smile seldom. And yet Cassius, to whom little credit is given by the others, is the brains behind the revolution; the man who persuaded Brutus to join the conspirators and who was right about the tragic progress of the whole affair. Was it not he who advocated that Antony should die with Caesar? How right he was, if the revolution was to succeed. Was he not right to try to dissuade Brutus from allowing Antony to speak at Caesar's funeral? Was he not right to dissuade Brutus from marching to Philippi? But if Cassius has a greater sense of realism and a keener perception than Brutus, he lacks the heroic proportions of his brother conspirator. He is doomed to play the part of the back-room planner who follows the leader whom he himself appointed, knowing him to be wrong, but knowing, too, that he himself has not the power to lead the cause.

Mark Antony

In direct antithesis to Cassius is Antony. We see him first stripped for the course, an athlete, a gamester, a lover of wine and song and, in a later play, of women too. In historical fact Antony was Consul at the time of Caesar's death, and a strange situation it must have been, when the head of the state, almost the equivalent of the President of the United States, stripped himself naked and ran round with the boys whacking the matrons of Washington who had failed to produce children.

I don't think the young, stoic, Julius Caesar would have set much store by Antony. But when Caesar returned from his campaigns, wise and disillusioned, he found Antony and his sporting outlook preferable to the narrow envy of Cassius and the puritans. Shakespeare, despite his pretence, was no Roman. He was bound to see the situation in Rome through Renaissance eyes, and however hard he tried to make his characters into true Romans, the Elizabethan inside him was bound to break out, nowhere more so than in the character of Antony. It is because Shakespeare was bound to see the Romans through the eyes of an Elizabethan that the costumes designed for this production show a hint of the Renaissance below the Roman togas, for we cannot escape from this invented world of Renaissance-Romanism that Shakespeare uses.

Antony is the Elizabethan gallant, the Earl of Southampton perhaps, if Brutus is Raleigh the philosopher. Such identifications are useless except in so far as they express the spirit in which they are conceived. Antony, then, is the brilliant but unreliable aristocrat loyal to Caesar who is his prefect, but utterly unscrupulous in his dealings with others. He is a sportsman and a gambler, prepared to take all on the throw of the dice, courageous, cruel and shrewd but no intellectual. He does not think things out like Brutus and Cassius, he relies on instinct and impulse. It is not so much love of Caesar which inspired Antony in the Forum, as the excitement of the gambler battling against odds. It would not be right, however, to discount Antony's achievement on that occasion by attributing his success merely to a gambler's luck. Antony wins the crowd over by sheer brilliant oratory. Unlike Brutus who appeals to the crowd's intellect, Antony appeals to their hearts. But it is when the odds are against him that Antony is at his best. The case is proved again in a later play. His impulsive character has neither the stability nor the honesty of Brutus, and his unscrupulousness is seen not only in the way in which he deliberately makes use of Brutus's generosity to turn the crowd against Brutus, but in his cynical handling of Lepidus and his falsification of Caesar's will.

I do not wish this part to be played in the heroic mould. Too often the actors who have chosen it have looked only at the grief over Caesar's body and the heroics in the Forum and seized on these pieces of rhetoric to draw the audience's sympathy. Antony is a cynic who profits by the situation of Caesar's death. He loves Caesar, but he was not above using his death as an opportunity for obtaining personal power. When his tears are shed for the dead Caesar, note how he receives the news that Octavius is arrived in Rome; how quickly he turns this to his advantage. It is Antony, not Brutus, who incites the people to revolution:

'Friends, Romans, Countrymen, lend me your ears.
I come to bury Caesar, not to praise him . . .'

What magnificent hypocrisy! With what skill—and let this be shown in the action—he withholds the contents of Caesar's will, tantalizing his audience with the promise of this secret information that he is not at liberty to tell them. Finally he lets them have it. He watches them rise to the bait and he leaves the Forum well knowing the mischief he has caused. And then comes the sequel; a man is killed, lynched by the mob—an innocent man—not the only one, but a symbol of what is to come. With this scene, the death of Cinna the poet, we will end the first part of our production. The curtain should fall on the flames of a burning Rome, as they flicker on the mangled limbs of the first of many victims of the dogs of civil war.

After this there is little to say about Antony. He behaves with gallantry towards his defeated opponents; he pronounces a generous Roman oration over the dead Brutus, but he has in fact met his match in Octavius Caesar and the interest in him is shifted over to this rising sun of Rome.

Octavius Caesar

Octavius says little, but the spotlight must dramatically move over to him. Here is the new Caesar, a young Napoleon rising out of the ashes of the rebellion and recreating in a new form the past which has been destroyed. Octavius is ice-cold in his disputes with Antony, but unmistakable is the impression he leaves. Here is the new Caesar reaping the benefit of the work of other men. For this reason I am deliberately doubling the part of the elder Caesar with that of his nephew. Who knows if Burbage's company did not also find this a convenient and effective economy?

A Symphony of Men

Julius Caesar is above all a play of men, but it would take too long to detail the characteristics of each one. There is scarcely a part in the play, however small, which does not bear its own distinctive colour, its small but effective signature in the great symphony. We note the dry irony of Cicero contrasted with the wild night of storm and mysterious omens, the pathetic poet Cinna answering the bestiality of the mob, the cynicism of Casca set against the high-minded sentiments of Brutus and Cassius. It is by such contrasts as these that the characterization of the smaller parts achieve their effect.

Casca is indeed a part contrasted within itself and presents a problem of consistency to the actor who plays it. The problem is how to marry the humorous, cynical Casca of the first appearance with the terror-struck appearance in the storm. Has Shakespeare made a mistake and merged two separate characters into one? If so it is the actor's job to try and reconcile them, bearing in mind that the cynic is often a poseur and can be the first to crack in a moment of terror. We should note that the soothsayer is one of those strange eccentrics endowed with second sight who help to build the tension of Shakespearian tragedy; that Strato is the honest compaigner who sleeps through defeat and performs his duty to his old commander without question but not without feeling; that Artemidorus is a strange Greek philosopher who having come by some knowledge of the impending plot makes a dramatic but ineffective attempt to inform Caesar of the danger; that Decius is a smooth-tongued flatterer of Caesar who successfully plays the hypocritical part of persuading Caesar to go to the Capitol. We should make a contrast between the two Tribunes, Flavius and Marullus, the one mild, the other masterful; we should show the individuality of each one of the conspirators and how their characters are exposed in the raw when faced with their terrible tasks. We should see to it that Messala, Lucilius, Titinius, and the common soldiers who follow Brutus and Cassius to Philippi has each one a character to contribute to the battle tapestry of the last act.

Finally, we must be sure that the crowd, one of the most important characters in the play, makes its proper contribution. This crowd is of course made up of small individual characterizations, like all crowds are—but such characterizations are not individually drawn by Shakespeare, with the exception of the Cobbler, and Shakespeare purposely refrains from writing his crowd characters as individuals, for it is more important to see the crowd as a body working by its own corporate motion than to be side-tracked by too much detail. The actors, therefore, who appear in this crowd must refrain from doing more than sketching in character lightly. They should concentrate on working as a team and represent the character of the crowd as a single body. There is ample evidence in this and other plays that Shakespeare despised a crowd of common people. This does not mean that he despised the low-born fellow as an individual, but he distrusted the unthinking multitude, the many-headed hydra which could be swayed this way or that by any loud mouthed fellow who addressed it. In the first scene of the play when we see this crowd in holiday mood, we are shown at once how fickle it is: at one moment celebrating Caesar's triumph over Pompey, and the next creeping away ashamed, when reminded of how it had celebrated the recent triumphs of Pompey. But the real character of the crowd is shown in the Forum scene and in the lynching of Cinna the poet. In the former we are struck by the ironical humour of the crowd's shifting loyalties; in the latter we see the full horror of revolution, the uncontrolled bestiality of a pack of hounds in full cry.

The Ladies

Neither Portia nor Calpurnia have any influence over the play's story for this is predominantly a male symphony, but both contribute much to its light and shade. Portia is a true patrician's wife; loyal, respecting her husband's humours, but, being a wife and one who is also in love with her husband, she requires him to share his cause of grief with her and by so doing relieve his troubled mind. The quiet beauty of Portia, her dignity and simplicity, her Roman pride at being Brutus's wife and Cato's daughter, and her gentleness and depth of feeling give a human touch to the character of Brutus which is much required. She acts like balm on this mind which is rent by contending loyalties and she shows us a Brutus who is great in commanding such a love as hers.

If Portia commands our love, Calpurnia commands our sympathy. Here is a wife no less anxious than Portia for her husband's safety, but a wife who can never command her husband's secrets, nor share his life. She is haunted by fears and superstitions; she does not possess Portia's courage, nor her quiet, gentle ways; she is married to a man whom she cannot hope to understand and to whom she can be very little use, for Caesar is self-sufficient on his pedestal. To Caesar she is something to be humoured. Seeing her to be more than usually moved by her fears, and being a superstitious man himself, Caesar yields to her entreaties not to go to the Senate, but once his pride is touched by Decius's subtle taunts, Caesar changes his mind and brushes her aside.

Portia and Calpurnia are quickly swept aside in this great brassy symphony of men, but the sweetness of the harp and the melancholy of the 'cello which they contribute are not without their effects.

The Last Act

The fall of Caesar which constitutes the subject of this play also brings about the climax of its drama; what follows might very well be anticlimax were it not for the fact that Shakespeare had a purpose and that purpose is, as we have said, to show us that political assassination, although well intended, is morally wrong. The effectiveness with which the tables are turned on the conspirators in the Forum scene keeps the play spinning along to the end of the third act. The hint of trouble between Octavius and Antony and the latter's unscrupulous behaviour towards Lepidus shifts the sympathies back to Brutus and Cassius who otherwise would be in danger of losing the game too easily for the play's good. The quarrel between Brutus and Cassius and the humanity of their reconciliation keeps our sympathies nicely balanced up to the end of Act IV. The difficulty of production lies in the last act, where we have little but the clash of battle and a tricky series of suicides to hold the interest. A great deal must therefore depend on the speed and vigour with which this battle is performed and the humanity which can be infused into it. By the time they reach the field of battle Cassius certainly, and Brutus probably, have a premonition of defeat. Their cause has turned sour, for Caesar dead is found to be more powerful than Caesar living, and the liberation that the conspirators had planned is changed to bloodshed and civil strife. What remains, then, is their courage in the face of failure and the preservation of their honour to the end. On the shoulders of these two men must lie the human sympathy that can be extracted from the last act. We must see them shouldering their intolerable burden with a brave face, encouraging their soldiers and inspiring in them the nobility and courage which are the particular characteristics of these mistaken, but honourable men.

POSTSCRIPT

The difficulty about *Caesar* is the crowd, not the crowd of Act I, which is purely a noisy, jubilant assembly, but the crowd of changing moods in the Forum scene. There are some producers who revel in crowd scenes, inventing brilliant cameo sketches, and intricate, weaving movements. Stanislavsky relates how, when he produced the play at the Moscow Arts Theatre, a whole cross-section of the life of ancient Rome was shown on the stage; armourers, merchants, matrons, patricians, courtesans and slaves filled the Forum with an ever-changing kaleidoscope of colour and movement. I cannot relate this treatment to Shakespeare's play, but that may just be that I am not very good at marshalling such mammoth spectacles.

I believe the crowd of *Julius Caesar* should not be broken up into details, but should behave as one body. If once you start to characterize individuals and load those individuals with business, the eye of the spectator will wander from the speakers and their hypnotic effect, which must work no less in the audience than on the crowd, is lost.

I consider that the only point the producer has to make is to show how fickle, unreliable and potentially terrifying is this many-headed hydra. My intention in this production was to mount the tension up to a white-hot climax, so that the Forum scene could flow into the final horror of the lynching of Cinna, the poet, and the curtain fall on the flames of a burning Rome. In this intention I believe we succeeded. The climax of the act as the crumpled carcase of Cinna lay deserted in the red glow of the fire and the songs and shouts of the maddened mob disappeared in the distance was, I believe, effective. But we suffered much pain in arriving at our goal.

At an early stage of rehearsals the crowd was in fine trim, but they were always two jumps ahead of Mark Antony. Not only did they tend to drown him with their noise, but they were inclined to sway him, instead of he them. The reason for this was obvious; the crowd's part is comparatively simple, whereas Mark Antony's is considerably difficult. The actor of Mark Antony will inevitably take longer to arrive at his performance than the crowd. But then, when Mark Antony was ready for action, the crowd's reactions dwindled to insignificance. The carefully arranged cues for shouts and yells either passed unnoticed, or a half-hearted cheer was raised by a particularly keen young actor, which sounded like a sneeze in an archbishop's sermon. What had gone wrong? The producer and the actor are two different people and although producers should tell actors what the broad effect of a speech must be, they should not tell them how to achieve it; that is what the actor is paid for. By marking so carefully in my prompt box these cues for the crowd's reactions, I was in fact telling Mark Antony how to speak his lines. But the actor of Mark Antony could not speak the speech as I had seen it. His climaxes were there, but they were in different places. His effect was what I wanted, but he achieved it in his own way. Consequently the poor crowd was completely lost.

The fault was mine; in my desire to put shape into the scene I had started to produce it at the wrong end. No matter how dull it may be, the producer must keep his crowd waiting until the principal actors are ready. I take this opportunity of paying tribute to the patience of the crowd, whose labours had to be laboriously reconstructed.

And, in this last postscript, may I also add my tribute to the patience of all actors and actresses who are doomed to suffer from the mistakes of a producer.

DATE DUE
